To:

MW00720843

Donald

On the backs
of
seahorses' eyes

Other books by DON CAUBLE

Poetry
Inside Out
early morning death fragments
Three on Fire
I am the one who walks the road / A selection of poems
    by Douglas Blazek, Tom Kryss, Don Cauble,
    with poem-drawings by Linda Neufer
On a hair-pin curve just under a blonde's left eye

Prose
This Passing World / Journey From a Greek Prison

On the backs of seahorses' eyes:
Journey of a man through time
Also known as *Book Four*

§

new & selected poems
and other storybook tales
1962—2012
by
Don Cauble

Don Cauble (signature)

introduction by
Tom Kryss

foreword by
Audy Meadow Davison

DANCING MOON PRESS
NEWPORT. OREGON

On the backs of seahorses' eyes
copyright © 2013 by Don Cauble

ISBN paperback: 978-1-937493-38-7
ISBN hardcover: 978-1-937493-39-4
ISBN eBook: 978-1-937493-40-0
Library of Congress Control Number: 2013934677
Manufactured in the United States of America

Cauble, Don
On the back of seahorses' eyes
1. Poetry; 2. Short stories; 3. Storybook tales. I. TITLE.

Book design: *Carla Perry, Dancing Moon Press*
Cover art: *Tom Kryss*
Cover design & production: *Jana Westhusing, StudioBlue West*
Back cover author photo: *Jane Speerstra*

DANCING MOON PRESS
P.O. Box 832, Newport, OR 97365
541-574-7708
www.dancingmoonpress.com
info@dancingmoonpress.com

First Edition

Author's note

Be not deterred by the length of this book. Simply read a poem or two, if it pleases you, then ponder upon the thoughts and feelings these words may have inspired within you, and then put the book aside for another day.

As for the stories in this book, are they real or imagined?
All stories are fiction, even true ones.

In grateful acknowledgement

In times gone by, some of these poems, in various forms, have appeared in the following daring and underground-breaking small press publications:

ACID/ Neue amerikanische Szene; ampersand; Analecta; Blazek-Edelson Anthology; Broken Cobwebs; Costmary Press; Death Row; entrails; Lung Socket; Peace Among the Ants; stones tongues pools running brooks; Thee Tight Lung Split Roar Hums; Thee Flat Bike #1; The Willie; Tansy; 48th Street Press.

Special thanks to **Audy Meadow Davison** for permission to publish "Flight of spirit," and "What happens when I read poetry." All rights to these works belong to Audy Meadow Davison.

And special thanks to **Lo Caudle** for permission to publish her poem, "It's Your Birthday: November 30, 2009." All rights to this poem belong to Lo Caudle.

In the presence of death, my mind has reached its limit and found a new freedom. Disillusioned, I rediscover a deep form of hope. Hope, as opposed to illusion or optimism, is not a prediction of things to come, nor is it redemption from something my small ego considers dreadful, nor is it a special knowledge revelation of a hidden future. To hope is to finally recognize the limits of my ability to comprehend the Power that has, is, and will bring all that is into being. Beyond that, all I can do is trust that inexhaustible mystery we all touch when we discover our spirit provides our best clue to the nature of Being.

Remember to look for a heaven in a wild flower, and an eternity in an hour.

Larry Setnosky
Friend, teacher, artist, carpenter
and fellow traveler
4/10/1940 — 2/25/2010

§

One becomes two, two becomes three,
and out of the third comes the One as the fourth.
Maria Prophetissa
Third century alchemist

Contents

Remembrance of you
Journey to Greece
1972-1975

Total fire, at last
1975-1981

Going into the darkness
1981-1985

This something-in-movement
Or, CrazyMan Returns to Mother's Arms
1987-1995

Endless the beginning
1996-2005

Looking out my kitchen window at the cemetery
2006-2010

Late thoughts
Where did the morning go?
2011-2012

Considering Don Cauble

In June 2004, I came across several of Don Cauble's poems in a pile of publications passed along by the poet and publisher Matthew Wascovich. At the time, I hadn't heard from Don in many years and the sight of the wonderful poems prompted me to contact Wascovich to convey my excitement. Matthew Wascovich provided me with Don's email address and, after 27 years, we were again talking. One of the forms these communications took, and to bring each other up to date, was the emailing of poems back and forth between our respective screens in Ohio and Oregon. For the most part, they were works by other poets—poems that for one reason or another had stuck in our hearts over time like a series of arrows. We broke off the shafts, so to speak, and exchanged them over the internet, without much explanation or comment. Within days, my email box was overflowing with poetry and I received via postal mail a typescript copy of Don's *On the backs of seahorses' eyes* and began reading it without taking the time to assume a seated position. From the first words, it was easy to see that Don's own poems were every bit as remarkable as those he admired by others. There were warm, philosophical letters to friends, stories from the work farm and prison in Greece, acts of magic performed by the stars over the Aegean, meditations on love and the wave—all from the perspective of a man who constantly questioned his own need to set into words the thousands of poems lived and experienced in the course of a day. In a poem dated from Corfu in the seventies, Don wonders whether he will ever again see the Oregon rain. The Oregon rain. How does it differ from the storm on Olympus? By the time I had ingested this tour de force of samsaric travel, I was again standing firmly on both of my legs, as it was the only possible position from which to launch a salute. Returning to the lawn chair in front of the early generation Dell, I had the odd pleasure of opening up an email from Don that included, in attachment, a high-resolution photograph of a galaxy. In Don's "A Single Flame Lights the Universe," he witnessed, gazing into the night, the death of a star, and in the accompanying instant his field of vision segues to the woman sleeping beside him.

Now it is the summer of 2012 as I read the current version of this book, and it is again late at night. Don's words, the ongoing product of a life of contemplation and engagement with the moment is, to me, a staggering record of one man's commitment to the human spirit—glow, as soft, as textured, as the map of the sea in a seahorse's eyes.

Tom Kryss, June 2004—July 4, 2012

Flight of the spirit

by Audy Meadow Davison

I've been thinking about people like flocks of birds—you know how they will suddenly fly into a tree, first a few and then the whole flock, and stay, dancing around, and then one will fly and then another, and then the whole flock except for a few. I've been thinking about people that way. A generation comes in and we dance around here on earth, chatting and flirting with each other and one of us will fly, and then a few more, and then almost the whole generation, just a few are left. It seems like our generation has started to fly. How do we choose when to follow?

What happens when I read poetry

by Audy Meadow Davison

it is simple to slip on the silk garment
that we call life, even though the world
we pass through is always turning it into
a rough cloth or something synthetic, artificial
and unhealthy. Still the morning is clear,
and at night, the stars can almost be seen
through the light daze of the city. Even the
sidewalks grow moss and weeds. If we pay
attention, life keeps calling us. Even our busy
days give way to sleep and the dreams that
speak in different languages, images and
emotions. Even our own minds return over
and over, if we let them, to forgetfulness.
And our bodies talk to us in pleasure and well
being, they talk to us in stiffness and pain.
Isn't that enough? What are we seeking?
Moments of simple joy arrive and disappear.
Pain comes and goes. Who knows where? Who
knows why? Who do we think we are? And
through all our tomorrows, life keeps calling.

Portland, Oregon
Spring 2012

16

On the backs of seahorses' eyes

§

Journey of a man through time

Before the beginning

1962-1965

§

Which of us has not remained forever prison-pent?
Which of us is not forever a stranger and alone?
Remembering speechlessly, we seek the great
forgotten language,
the lost lane-end into heaven,
a stone, a leaf, an unfound door

—Thomas Wolfe, *Look Homeward, Angel*

§

all which isn't singing is mere talking

—e.e. cummings

Lost words

Where are the lost words that drag my heart
deep, deep into your shallow arms?
Lost words that drag upon my heart.
Sounds that speak your eyes.
Lost voices muffled by the noisy throb
of your steel
and concrete heart.
Somewhere in the hot Georgia night
a pretty girl with soft slurred voice
laughs
as the lightning flashes.
Somewhere on a ragged beach, two young lovers kiss.
A sob catches in the girl's throat.
Then, silently, they wade into the ocean.
The water crawls onto the shore
and washes their proud sure footprints
into lost time.
Lost words.
Lost sounds.
A passing glance through a car window.
Warm sparking eyes seek the wanderer's face,
they promise him life and love forever and ever
until the morning,
if only....
Browned grasses that bend beneath the October wind.
A girl dressed in a yellow two-piece suit
lies upon a small rotted wharf. She watches the waves
until she drowns.
Where have the words gone?
Lost words. Lost voices.
Books lie scattered in the mind
like clusters
of dead leaves,

21

like dry, rustling wind-sounds.
A college boy searches for a lost chord
on a cheap guitar.
He thinks of a girl with aureoles
of sun-warmed hair.
A girl with freckles across her nose and cheeks
stammers, There is a god.
A boy with unruly hair takes his hand from her blouse
and answers, There is no god.
Lost sounds.
Lost voices in the night.
Lost voices that drag upon my heart.

January 1963

Yes, isn't it pretty to think so?

for Brett

Why do you come
to me
hiding in your Jewish
hair
& your crayon
dreams?

My hands grow
hungrily
into your thin
bones.

Your hair is a
fountain,
your green eyes
small fish
darting
into my blood.

On a golden chain,
a green stone
dangles
on your neck.

You take
off
your clothes.

Your eyes are green!
Green

23

Transformations, Diabolical Urges &
Divine Inspiration

1965—1972

§

Come forth, young poet, and rage against the lies
and deceptions of this world, and seek
always to remember
who you are!

§

I crash thru broken eyeglasses,
the Golden Disc fear and desire.
Her Marilyn Monroe faces melts,
dripping candles into my hands.
from *Visions*, 1967

We begin with the sun

The orange light flashes,
you cross the street,
your high-heeled steps
a jazz legato
moving you to-
wards me,
wind on grass—
in my mind
a rain goddess,
your short green coat
a forest,
your eyes
beds
of
     hotwet
leaves

How beautiful your legs!
I thought,
wanting to drink
in
your wetness

Then we smiled
and brushed
past
each other

forever

3 night letters

Mr President

Is it true
when men die
they die forever,
even in war?

Mr. President

Is it true
French philosophers
claim death comes at dawn,
that even our dreams yawn
from lack of sleep?

Mr. President

Is it true
God has never seen
how a man dies?

Death, too, is a game people play

I remember watch-
ing my father
whip my brother
— Jack was 10
and I was 7—
with a limb
stripped of its leaves
from a backyard peach
tree.

I wept
& clenched my fists
into knives,
my stomach trembling
in rage
& silence.

All that summer
I waited
    & swore
someday
I would kill my father.

Now I know
both of us

must
die.

Even God must be lonely at night

even in the dark the blond girl could hear the
legs of the fuzzy spiders crawling over the
walls. she could hear soft fuzzy plops! as
they fell from the ceiling onto the floor.
     the blond girl sat on the edge of her
bed. she listened. breathing. she could
hear their breathing. like muffled canticles,
she thought. outside, she could hear soft
rain. she could hear the rain and the soft
wet crawling of the spiders. they came down
the walls onto the floor. the girl lay on the
bed and waited. if she stirred too quickly,
she could frighten them away. last night
she had frightened them. but tonight, slowly, so
slowly, her blond fingers touched cold buttons. one
arm. then the other. her breasts were naked. white.
even in the dark. white. she shivered. the spiders
crept closer. like prayers over wet lips, she thought.
she knew they were watching her. she could not see
them. but she knew they were waiting.
     the girl slipped her small hands down
below her belly. gently she drew up her
knees and slid the pajama pants from her legs
and body. she closed her eyes and touched small
hands to her wiry blond nest. now the spiders had
crossed the room. without seeing them, she knew
they had reached the bed. she could hear their soft
wet prayers. she could feel their fuzzy legs slowly
crawling and crawling. crawling up her legs. crawling

After the Wipe-Out Gang
come the Keepers

Inside the eye a mouth scream.
Inside the mind an i is stolen:
capitalized: spiked and dropped.
Four lumberjacks tag-team trees
inside your head,
you stick out your hands to fight
and draw back to swing and wonder
why the Local Gang Leaders
are laughing and calling you Nubby.
You watch yourself strangling inside
shoe strings,
as ice cold blades
slice you into bite size
and a woman's voice tells you
to drag your split balls off her teeth;
and all the time Dali's watches
are gumming your heart into a clot
but you keep pushing the Rock
toward the top as you discover
too late your hands are taped.
You look at your watch and light a smoke
as words pounds nails into stones
and every blow scrapes your skin
and hangs it in the wind,
and you begin to wonder
how far you can fall,
and if Rimbaud is really dead,
as the log rhythms smash together
and your name is printed
in glowing Roman numerals
which the Marquee Girls dust

each hour upon hour.
And, then, during the night
as the Nuns sleep,
some men with ladders and bad spelling
and nothing to do
come and scramble the stars
into an obscene joke.

All night the river flows

November leaves rattle under
my feet, the street light
flashes WALK.
I cross, holding
these words to you
in my hands,
a flower
in my heart,
a flower
in the Buddha's
hand, true
as a red rose;
as you lie sleeping
in bed
next to your husband,
you dreaming me
touching you;
my hands, an ache
to recognize you,
at last,
my hands, all
that I am,
a man in love,
a kindness in the dark;
your blonde skin
a promise of light;
my hands, touching
you, moving
over the round,
lovely moons of your
breasts and pale
blue-sky veins

that flow
beneath your white
skin, and down
into the warm,
blonde opening inside you,
your body a golden ring
into which
I slip my finger,
my mouth
kissing wet
circles
split by your
nipples,
blonde hair between
my lips,
blonde legs under
and over mine.

2
I'm walking and it's cold
I'm dreaming of dying
The leaves taste sweet
in my mouth
They rattle as I step

3
Drowning, I think,
must be a long way to walk

Love outside the asylum

Letters from Jamie Brown

The dog directs the mast of the hunt, she wrote.
It is over for me.
They cut open my head.
Two flowered dresses red blue,
one backwards over a robe,
one pall mall in pocket wheeeee....
A negro nurse dragging me down the hall.
FOLLOW THE NURSE!
FOLLOW THE NURSE!
Bring her to our spiritual meeting,
say blue uniform guarding doors.
Think! The other side!
I was to go but through what door?
In the tub room? Naked? What was I to do?
I wash and wash and wash.
I am still dirty.
I am not clean!
Later, I sit feet dangling from bed.
Were you coming to get me?
I lie down, dream.

2

When I was seventeen, she wrote,
I went to Boston,
alone in a dirty green room.
I fell in love with a homosexual.
He lived across the hall.
We walked along the Charles
in autumn rain,
crystalling orange burnt leaves
against iron fences.
La Jetee', will I ever forget that damn movie?

The pills, they do nothing.
I wanted to take the whole bottle, but didn't.
They would not kill me.
What do they do, David?
These people dressed and perfect in appearance.
How do they live? Where?
Trees, the music says trees
and air and birds and
GARBAGE,
purple pansies.
I wonder who in the hell
ever believed the music,
writing it
and making a bunch of fat old peasants
sit in wonder and paying pennies?
Oh, David, I am so happy!
I will read and be well one day.
I WON'T DIE BECAUSE I DON'T WANT TO!
There are kids who fish and throw away
what they catch
and what they aren't going to eat,
but, by Christ, I believe,
and if there was a fish jumping in the pail,
and if he was still jumping
after I walked six miles,
I'd personally walk back and let him swim.

3

In Eugene, last spring,
she wrote,
I saw three birds,
fallen while in midst
of self-imposed hypnotic states.

I knew them to be placed there
for me, dressed in monk's camel coat
and off-white levis,
hunched on corner bench
in view of the fountain,
blooming fuchsia flowers.
Then later at the pot shop,
"It really isn't very good,
it has a hole in it
and the glass is bubbly..."
and the giant sized one
with the funny whiskers,
who in a photo wore a beret,
and on the night I saw him:
"You feel so Goddamn much.
You bleed all over the street,
I've seen you!"
And I, standing there,
knowing nothing to be done.

The girls, she said,
today the girls
were tossing their kitten
in a cheesecloth curtain
given for some unreason by the landlady.
My seeing them and as it is
and what they did
and them singing lullabies
thinking it doesn't hurt
and because its voice isn't very loud
hanging the cat up as mistletoe
in the form
of a hummingbird's nest.
"And never hurt a cat in anger,"

they said,
while driving it insane,
so it will never know the outside
and be frightened to leave.

No one is ever wise, David,
but becomes ageless,
becoming ageless,
David, we don't grow old,
just die.

4

Oh, David, it is no use.
I have no strength,
no mind.
They hurt me.
They loved me so much,
they wouldn't let me go.
They killed me.
And when I awoke
there was a gray stone wall
and I couldn't withstand it.
I couldn't fight.
I couldn't hit them.
I can't hate, I can't.
SHIT! I hate the word;
there are worse.
Vulgarity. Garbage
not worth the heave to the truck.
Scream it.
SEND ME TO THE SCREAMERS!!!!!

Somewhere between streets
& asylum wax-stocked
girlflesh
torments
& wet eye focuses

Time is a child, said Heraclitus,
& we're playing his game.
Is it Hide & Seek?
Blind Man's Bluff?
Red Rover, Red Rover,
send the lovers right over?
Ring around the roses,
a pocket full of holes?

We spackle the god
within us—
he can't escape!
Naked with only sunglasses
he hides to dodge our
Instamatic Eyes,
his hands knotted & tied to
exploding tracks.
Our souls slapped to ceilings
of the body,
our eyes tooth-picked with death,
our heads slam the wall:
we scream: I'LL KILL YOU!

We strangle door knobs,
wrestle shoe strings,
and, winning,
congratulate ourselves.

We strip to a fist of hair,
and eyes like frantic mouths
catsuck the open souls
of our being.
We push water & land through
sun into plant,
into fish,
into crawling snails--
& already with horns.
We stare at the Hemingway bull,
unaware of the blade's red scream,
the obscene roses & peek-a-boo
nipples of ghost madonnas.
Our heads ripped to quick graves,
we hang to concrete curbs
& wonder how to stand higher
than the blades.
We stab each other into holes,
and this time we think the last time
but too soon her fingers feel you
up & down,
she fits your body into her hands
& stripteases your mind
into flashes of night & day
& you're trying to ask WHO?
—as the safety razor falls at dawn
& neatly slices the face
from your hands.

You push a button & clam-
lock the doors,
but the walls are mesh,

your flesh embarrassed,
caught at playing naked
& wanting to crawl inside
to stop up the holes,
like cramming keys to make words,
to make sense,
or just to hide all the empty no-returns,
as animals & gods fight in
the open ring of your hands;
& you standing & watching &
wondering what the fuck
you're doing
& why
& how come you
didn't do it sooner.

Leda strips down for swans,
& men die.
Cats stretch in the sun.
Women roll over in dreams
& the moon makes love to a cloud.

We whisper & we're alone
with ying-yang fingers:
they're slowly closing into a fist,
& when we go rushing in
there's no flash...only aloneness.

Cars move straight
like
over streets
and I'm moving
toward

Fuzz is hip.
Fuzz slips a note
under the door
BANG! YOU'RE DEAD!
& Our Hero has
already
ripped the sink,
the dresser,
the bed,
& junked them for $24
& now boards himself
behind shut lids
cause he also is hip
& he is hip to Fuzz
the crutch we hobble on
cause it's the hard way
to walk
& we're hung up
on the Dead Man's noose
the bits of Porsche
mangled in our flesh.
We hear the grass walk
toward us,
we hear the ground quake
throwing stones above
our heads
& we hide to dodge

but they pound us
into the ground
PAY YOUR RENT OR GET OUT!
& inside his tomb
the Old Man screams
FUCK YOU! I AIN'T DEAD!
& they rip the mimeo doors
into clubs,
they slap our words
like baseballs
& we crash into beer cans
that EXIT us
thru scoreboards
into fans
waiting
for the Big Hit
for the Home Runner
the Slam Play
the Hero of the Hour.
& each 7 years
the Stones come stalking
they carry signs
HURRY UP PLEASE
IT'S TIME!
& the Son wakes screaming
THE OLD MAN IS DEAD!
THE OLD MAN IS DEAD!
& Olympia billboards
It's the water!
& I say aren't you Carbon
cause Blue Print keeps
rubbing my hands

& he says, well then don't touch
& I say, why don't you
& he interrupts, I have
already
the jokes on you
Chicken Little,
here comes the crack-up!
& I say bunchingmywords
which way is OM?
& he answers, Eastern air lines
HOME
& I say, YOU aren't Bogart
not even Mordor!
& he says, how about that!
Now what you gonna do?

Come on in, she said to me

I walk 70 blocks thru a cemetery
and pick flowers
from which
beautiful skulls will grow.

The second-hand lady opens her door.
I'm standing on the steps with a nervous smile
and the skull of an angel in my hands.

She shows me to the basement,
to a small darkened room with a thousand walls
and a shifting mirror;
a room where her husbands never go.
She hides the skull under the stairs,
then she takes off her shirt and faded jeans.
Sometimes, she tells me, they just forget I'm here.

Next morning, she keeps watch thru a broken widow.
Trucks are in the street, she warns me.
The trucks have loud speakers.
Her husbands are searching the closets.
Cops are outside with rubber hoses.
They throw up barricades.

I disguise myself as a man.
They never see me.

Inside you
whispering
thru shut sockets
and circling light
dreams

Our voices cut a freeway
& the Greyhounds come riding;
Dr. Sanpaku tells us
in 13 languages
how we're poisoning
inside Saviors,
the key gets stuck in the door
& you tell me the only way out
is to crawl inside.
I turn, take one step backwards
CRAAASH!
The backdoor went out the front,
you say.
You open the fire escape.
Broken trees jamlog your thighs,
snow waits for spring.
Go slow,
you tell me
& my fingers hear Picasso flowers
splitting your throat,
mouths open into skulls.
When will IT begin?
I asked,
as I stepped into the end.

Standing still

Saj, the Grave Keeper
hangs out with the ghost of a face.
He sticks his eyes
in backwards—
If I wasn't so serious,
he cries,
I'd laugh myself to death!
But you know how it is,
I've got to stick around
and take all this down.
Aarun, the first born,
crashes the doors;
he shouts to the Greyhounds:
Catch me if you can!
I only want to catch
what's behind me,
says Tom—
our hero in this story—
and presses his face
to the windows
that guard his soul.
They always told us
to follow a running stream
and, if possible, a railroad track,
but I just keep following myself.
Step inside...
says the Grave Keeper,
The most you'll get
is the least you can expect.

2

I watch the Mind Pickers
sorting Blue Giant into dwarfs
and the heavies play mystical chairs
with his unblinking eyes.
Floating Lady sighs,
I worry about coming
when I haven't even left....
It's all the same,
says One-Eyed Jane,
with a laugh that reminds me
of tinkling cymbals.
The Magician crosses himself
then disappears into a cloud
of dust
and old book covers
musty with names of famous poets.
Lady G. shoots her white horse.
He was just a dream, she says,
in a bitter tone out of tune;
a dream that belongs to a lover
I once knew.
Then she hops in bed
with her bodyguards, all seven,
as her lover hangs himself
with disbelief
and a decent man's
hidden desires and long buried
guarded pleasures.
Goldilocks hides in plastic bags,
she plays with herself

while her boyfriend complains
to the crowd,
I've been all around
but I can't find a way to get in!
Each night,
the Head Dealer looks out to a busted house.
I sure hope I'm being cheated,
he says to the crowd,
I'd hate to think I play this bad!

3

This must be a family plot!
cries Tom,
looking around at all the pictures
of himself hanging
on the walls
and a door guarded by dragons
of deceit.
Obviously,
I'm in the wrong place!
What? Are you leaving
so soon? whispers Becky.
You wanna refund, is that it?
He's beginning to catch on,
says the Keeper,
and smiles as warm as a light
in the window of a winter's day.
I think he wants out,
but in and out are dreams
of the past,
he says.

You see...for us...
there's only ourselves
and, he chuckles, these blasted mirrors.
Hey, and chewing gum!
Don't forget that's what holds this house
together,
that and the mirrors,
giggles One-Eyed Jane,
as she teases me
through peek-a-boo dresses and sly gestures
with her painted fingers
and a rose in bloom
tattooed
on her thigh,
next to Venus giving heads up to Jupiter.
Escape is useless, don't you see?
Go outside
and it's still raining.
She touches my hands
to her face
in the mirror and the rain,
What else is there to do...but look?

—

Deadwood with screaming roots

Vanessa stops with her skin;
there's no place to go.
The prisoner hangs to the ocean,
Grave robbers steal my eyes,
they bind them to the skies.
A ghost writes in water:
THIS IS WHAT YOU WANTED,
ISN'T IT?

Saj builds a fire inside the sea
and then turns the house inside out.
He gives free passages to the angels.
He writes on the walls:
You can go as far in
as you can go out.

Tom plays with the keys,
he sees the garden surrounded by dogs.
A cop shouts,
Well whacha waitin' for?

Aarun holds a burning spade.
I come closer and Vanessa cries, How?

2

The flower grows toward the sun,
the flower never asks, yet the flower
never misses.
Then come the Keepers with stones
in their hands.
They put up fronts and lock the doors.

If there's no one else,
we shoot holes through ourselves.
Ah, yes...smiles Lisa,
and goes upstairs to dress as a nude.

That's the way it goes, so they say:
First your money then your clothes.
It's all in your mind, anyway.
Yeah, I know...moans the prisoner.
That's why we're still here.

3

Tom runs screaming through the walls,
Let me in! Let me in!
In time...Becky whispers...in time.

There's nothing you can save

SOLAR ECLIPSE IN THE 5TH HOUSE

Invisible snakes punch holes in the ring,
I throw stones at the moon.
Brown birds freeze in skeletons
& I wait for Lisa to undress.
On the Creeper, she says,
you never know what time it is.
Bad days drive her to the edge,
she sleeps in her clothes
& I cannot hold her dreams.

THE SIGN SAYS 84

The middle-age priest bows
to an empty house,
He shows his hand to the audience
& then shouts, *Higher Mysteries!*
I keep getting higher
but I don't see any *mysteries.*
The workers clock out and go home,
They complain the day's a drag
& night's only a thin cover.
The prisoner keeps one eye hanging;
the eagle dies at the window
& the 5th horseman stalls at the gate.
Aarun works all hours making gloves.
If I slow up now, he cries, I'll stop!
Saj, who says he never takes life
personally,
turns every stone to a full house.
Tom swears it's too soon

& takes up automatic writing.
It's not what you know,
Saj warns him.
It's what you grow!

ALMOST...LIKE A GHOST

The Magician digs holes in the sky.
He cries to the sun:
I've done what you asked,
I've shown them my tricks!
What more do they want?

Vanessa looks out to a world on fire;
I burn incense to Mexico's ancient Queen
& dream dreams of falling rocks.
Vanessa sees through the smoke,
ghosts cling to the walls.
Looks tell you everything, she says,
if you know how to look.

The Grave Keeper turns my way.
He looks as far as the eye can see.
Step quickly...he says...
& in all directions...
then you'll know what I mean.
Is that all? I ask.
Sure...he replies and points to the walls....
But if you keep dragging those ghosts
around,
you'll only lose yourself
and wind up in a pigeon hole.

With one foot in the grave, the fool pauses & dreams he's dancing

Pigs set up house in the garden,
George the clean-up man
holds a long arm up his sleeve—
The whites of his eyes glint like stones.

The 7th daughter sleeps with the lights;
she spends her days taking baths.
The Magician empties his dark hat,
ghost rabbits jump the escapes.

Jane tells you she's from the other side
& can't get back through the traffic.
The wind blows lace curtains across your face.
You stare at the ceiling
& run your hands up the bare walls.

Remember how simple death used to be?

The fat king quickly claims
that nothing's really changed.
The second-hand lady brings me her kiss
but I'm stealing looks at the show.

Paranoid cops,
with orders from the street cleaners,
murder Cleveland's first prophet
with his own 22 vision.
Revolutionists kiss the air above his head
& wonder why the holes in his body
keep screaming.

The girl on the side hangs another rope
for the young train robber
one step ahead
of the blindfolded switchman.

The mad historian
crashes a burning time machine
through double rums
and back alleys
that curve into each other
like acid freeways flashing van Gogh exits.

The rebel son rips the stage door
from the horse's mouth.
He drops his pants
and the school girl shrieks—
she does not see her own clothes
disappearing.

The oldest living poet paints his eyes
and dresses the lion with terror.
He staggers under L. A. suns
with whores who won't give an inch,
as skinny, rich blondes play tricks
on his bravado sheets,
singing, O beautiful for spacious thighs.

The prison mystic out-waits the walls.
He steps from his body with a wink
then slashes the cord.
He takes his life into his own hands.

Gen. Opinion hangs out the window.
Buttons lob his ears,
Boy Scouts ape his wings.
He pokes one finger in his eyes
& the other up his ass,
then he shouts for the guards.

Oh, and just when the stars give up looking
for a light,
and firemen jam the street with their trucks,
and the 9 bring up the rear
with visions of transfiguration,
Lilly Bulero tags your shadow with his.
He dregs up the great U-shrinker
who bums the first corner in sight,
as he points to the sky, clapping
with thunder and smoke,
and quotes his favorite joke:
Here lies Blue Giant!

When you come to her door
empty handed,
and she tells you,
It's time to go

My sister lives in a dream,
she whispered,
with the skull of our father.

I smiled at her words,
as I paced the ceiling
& stared through the clothes in her hands.

I can be whatever you want! she cried.
I can show you the universe
in the space of an eye!

The house stood still.
Rooms closed like empty banks.
Skeletons leered from every bed.
Through disappearing walls
I could see a girl's thin body
wrapped in sheets like a corpse.

Husbands kissed her dead mouth,
Lovers flashed lights in her eyes.
Children hid in the flowers
and cried for her milk.

A priest mumbled from the law
and a judge pointed his finger at me.
What you took so long ago, he shouted,
now you must give back!

There was no place to hide.
My head pounded with fire,
I rushed the sky in anger.
The house dissolved into a veil of light.
I stood before a shrine
and a magician dressed me in purple.
In one hand, he showed me the sword
and in my left, a burning cup.
If you're looking for the way out,
he said, Come....
And he showed me into a room
concealed in the heart of the shrine.

I stared with horror and disbelief.
Men and women knelt in fear to the walls.
They tore and mutilated their organs
as they shouted oaths to love and power.
In the center, a man gazed into the light
with his hands chained to each other.
Three figures circled him with fire.
A lovely girl danced naked in his eyes.
Now do you see? said the magician.

The cup spilled to the floor,
the three figures vanished.
I rushed to set the man free
but the woman called my name;
and the sword in my hand
turned to a golden skull.

In a moment
you'll begin to suspect
who I really am

He wrote strange letters
to a woman
who ruled
the moon in her thighs
and he tried to say
when you've covered the sun
there's nowhere to go.
She painted lotuses over his ceiling
and exploded mines beneath his fingers.
Stand still and dance!
he cried to the shadows.
How can you dance
like a scorpion
dodging from room to room?
She lifted her blinds
and opened his eyes—
You must leave...she told him...
You've overlooked the sky
so very long....
NOT JUST NOW, he tried to explain
for his hands were empty
and his sleeves were bare.
His mind unraveled the past
for a place of his own
but the fire blazed at his back
...out there...OUT THERE....
Is there no place
you can hide?
He grabbed the lights
when she wanted the dark

and inside her house
an ocean gave birth
to a seahorse,
fire split the sky,
and he touched the moon
with hands like the lifting
of stones.

Death of the fly

The room was crowded.
Kabir, Bosch and Issa traveled without walls
and I was shown through inner circles.
In time, said Kabir,
all your questions will be answers.
So I poured more wine,
and then came a knock on the door.
The Magician entered the crowded room.
In his hands he carried a body.
No wonder you're late,
scowled Issa...
Dragging a corpse!
To others, the mind is a chain,
replied the Magician, looking wise,
but for me, it's a golden key.
Bosch remained silent.
He saw into the man's heart
and knew how he burned to free his mind.
This all seems so strange, I thought;
What about the body?
Splendid! cried Issa.
Ah...agreed Kabir, the night is chilly.
Even Bosch smiled.
The Magician understood
and turned, at once, into the fire.

The last man standing

The miser opened his jewels
and stared into a burning hole.
His wife lay on a couch of gold
and gazed into the open sea.
Men came and went
through her outer chambers,
where a sleeping princess
sang childhood songs to a golden serpent
that danced in her head
so no man could open her heart.
A priest kept the keys in his fist;
A judge with no mercy handed time
to the workers who froze in motion
each step of the way;
and within a cell,
no larger than his soul,
a man with one eye opened a hole
through the darkened sky.
On his chest, he painted a sun;
and over his genitals, he placed a throne.
On the throne,
a king waged a never-ending war
with his three sons;
for in his heart
a torch blazed for the princess,
but she feared his reason
and hid herself in the secret folds
of her golden couch,
where the serpent ate at her heart,
and the miser gathered the pieces
in his pocket
and offered them to his wife,

who laughed as the king died in her arms.
The priest swept the floors with his cross.
The judge threw his book to the fire.
The three sons emptied the sea in rage,
and inside a burning hole,
they found a poet with a golden key,
till at last,
with nowhere to go,
the one-eyed man opened his heart
and the jewels in his mind shattered to glass.

Out of the tomb, a child of light

For those still
in the Circle,
circling the sky

Here comes the sun

It wasn't power, It wasn't God, It was truth we
were looking for. Under our noses...inside our
heads...beneath the covers...between the sheets. Three
sheets in the wind. The wind that turns the Wheel of
Fortune and misfortune. The duality of experience as
seen thru the eyes: *vision, magic, and poetry.*

The Seeing Eye.
My poetry refuses to become anything more than
seeing. The eye catching the hand. The wheels on fire
burning lovely flowers that open the eyes. (Which
One?) Mystery, illusion, reality. It's all poetry, so what!
Zen, Magic, Maya, all fire!

Everything goes. Giving us the Gothic, Frank
Lloyd Wright, mountains and rivers without end.
Poetry wipes out the false bottoms, cleans away all
your ghosts, then sends you on the Way, laughing,
leaving those with telescopes peering into your dust
and circling the ashes.
Out we come, in we go.

Be high, be miserable, be whatever you want but
don't confuse it with the Way. Will you buy and sell
lost gold mines? Jerusalem Revisited...A Journey thru
Horrors and Other Joys. Or, I can't read this map!

Perhaps a Gurdjieff, a sudden shock, even a kiss, might wake the sleeping, but you can't wake the dead. (Give 'em a watch and they'll stop...always, always.)

The fire that remains

When you flow, there's no circle. Know that you and *It* are one. (It's name slips me.)

Just flow with It. It's the last word. Before birth. Then comes death only seconds later. (Do you disagree? Fine with me. This is the way, an ordinary day. This is no song, this is subterfuge...)

It's an old Indian trick, doing away with Time.

Far as the eye can see, far as the mind could Go— there's only truth, there's only poetry. Poetry is a matter of seeing, *naturally*. Abracadabra spelled out. The mind concrete.

The poet must kill himself each step of the way. That is, the image of himself. He must let go all ideas of self, the false gods, the elusive angels. He must show us where he is, TOTALLY, without gumming the air with fantasies, visions, or hallucinations. But don't confuse this dying with suicide. Will you take the ring for the gem?

The mind's a wonderful thing but don't mistake it for the moon.

The lower mind thinks, the Higher Mind sees, and this mind keeps both in hand. Tarot sees the Game but is Tarot a game? (No, she's a nice Lady who has a white cat named Tasha.)

66

Nice game she plays, Yes! No!

No wonder you can't see, you're always looking!
Everything depends on This.

You can look within and without. The man who
looks within is no wiser than the man who looks to the
trees, the stars, the cathedrals, for his God. To bring the
search within you is more sophisticated, to be sure. But
you're still looking. For something higher, something
separate, something other than you.

There's no higher hocus-pocus.

There's no need to mystify life. Life is mystery.
Don't listen to the Buddha. Look *thru* his words.
See the Yogi hold his breath and the Poet his nose.
Poems are tombstones for those on the way out.

Expanding the walls won't get you thru the
doors. *(There are no doors, there are no walls.)* You can't
afford to become a museum or a side show. Not with
backyards crumbling around you like crazy and the
Unknown waiting to blind you like a huge sun, *if you
stop to be blinded.*

Sort thru the leftovers, if you wish. There MIGHT
be some life. It's a little soon, you can't leave 'em just
yet. As you explain how Duty or the Law or
Investment keeps you chained to the past.

It's not fair!

Make this into an epitaph, only don't stop
moving. (It's nice to be moving, now there's nowhere
to go.)

Here lies...but then again!

Don't give up in despair, give up in Joy.
If you must give up....

West of east, full circle out

October returns and closes the earth.

I've come to you thru the fires.

There's no mind, no time, no space. There's no
Fool, no One to fool. The trap is illusion; freedom,
illusion.

Truth is both and…

You need one to conceive zero. (But whence
cometh the One?) *You are the one.*

The poem is shaped by a man's spirit, and comes
pulsing thru all his bodies, into consciousness.

The 3rd eye opens the sky.

I saw the eternal in the night, I saw this moment
in the light. (Two mirrors endlessly facing each other.)
There's no past, no future, we're only moving thru,
don't you see?

Remembrance of you
Journey to Greece

1972-1975

§

*In the beginning
there was you.
Then there was light
and I saw you.*
—David Pendarus
"The Delicate Ribbons of Light That We Are"

Author's Note: All the poems and prose selections in "Remembrance of you / Journey to Greece" first appeared in my novel, *This Passing World / Journey From a Greek Prison*; AuthorHouse, 2006.

Please visit <u>www.thispassingworld.com</u> to find out more about this novel.

Before

Before the breath,
there is you.
Before the 99 names
of the Essence,
before the Divine Mother,
before birth and death,
there is you.
Before time and space,
before earth, fire, air and water,
before the cosmos,
there is you.
Before you is the sea,
within you the road.
Before both sea and road,
there is you.

Monemvasia / 1972

I knew we would never meet again

*For Christine, white-skinned Swedish tempest
in a black dress and a voice like honey*

You wanted the center, but it gave you no peace.
You wanted my eyes, but they left you no reason.
I have seen the angel inside you,
ashen as your final transfiguration.
I have traveled your world with its smoke
and mechanical heart.
Still, your dark glance—blonde as the moon's edge—
took me in a moment.

Blame the ghost that unraveled the play.
Everyone dies in the end. Or so it seems.

Believe in the Fish: golden as myth;
more slippery than wet stones.
Believe in the stars and everything under the sun.
Believe in the Sea. Believe in the Self.
Believe whatever you want. It doesn't matter.

I hear yapping dogs in your teeth.
I see a magician's trick in your hands,
and I see your unfaithfulness at the drop of a hat.
I see your plunging neckline pinned to a veil,
and your unborn child in glass on a stone.
I see you in light and rock,
and in the middle of the road I see you.
In the fire and smoking eucalyptus leaves,
I see you;
and in the shadows,

and in the hours my love cleans house,
I see you.

But already you have merged as a dream
into my heart,
and I lie here in the dark,
a stranger to myself.

Greece, 1972

A single flame lights the universe

It is night.
A single flame lights the universe
and my love lies sleeping in the quietness of our room.
It is an immense room
in a timeless land by the sea,
and the air is warm and still, and only the light,
only the light softly covers her beauty.
I gaze into the night and milky-white galaxy.
I see a star dying in the vast calmness,
and my heart returns home,
without hesitation, but with joy,
and comes to rest in my love's moonlit arms
and in her gentle breathing.
My eyes gaze upon her beauty.
I look and look and am not filled.
(Her beauty is elusive, unborn; never will it be exhausted.)
I am breathless with her beauty.
I look and look and am not filled.
I see her playful treasures hidden in dreams
and gifts washed from the sea.
My love, she dreams as a child dreams
of green trees shining and shining
and of golden summers gathered in her hair.
The blue, jewel sky universe embraces my love,
rosy dawns awaken her,
and purple rim rainbows come to rest at her feet.
My eyes gaze upon her beauty.
I look and look and am not filled.

Bottoms up

Now, it's barely light outside. I'm in the kitchen with a warm blanket wrapped around me. Our little kerosene heater helps, but not much. I woke early and couldn't get back to sleep. I kept thinking of how every culture has created a myth to explain the origin of the world. The Greeks certainly had their turn at it. The Hindus, the Egyptians, the Chaldeans. the Semitic tribes, the Mayans, the Toltecs. None that I knew, however, satisfied me. The teller of the tale could explain the elephant holding up the world, but not the tortoise holding up the elephant. None could explain Before the beginning. Like the scientific Big Bang, they all began and ended in a lot of noise. Both the Great Cosmic Mother and the Father Warrior Creator had failed us. The time has come to heal this fracture and move on. Time for a new vision, a new language. A language that once more captures the essence, the heartbeat, the mystery. A process we could participate in, that would bring balance and wholeness into our lives; not a creation of distance and control and domination. But who am I to tell the tale of how the world came into being? I come from a cultural tradition that's mostly interested in the origin of money and power and how to keep score with it—not in the origin of self—if the "self" exists. Perhaps the self, too, is just another myth. Just our values at the moment; just our fluid, ever-changing— or rigid—beliefs; our likes and dislikes that come and go like buddhas on the cosmic sea. Somewhat like scientific truths. Science shackles itself to the edge of this planetary ship with self-measuring lines of timid consistency, afraid of falling over the edge. Most of the time anyway. And am I not like this myself? Longing to know the truth, but sticking like a barnacle to the familiar and comfortable and to what I can see and hear and smell? Lazy as a summer day, I am. Narcissistic as a full moon. Pompous, arrogant, full of pride. Ready at the drop of a hat to defend the rightness of my beliefs, the back of my neck bristling like a junkyard dog. As a lovely friend of mine (and a spiritual healer/teacher) once said to me in a fit of laughter and exasperation, "David, you're the most prideful motherfucker I've ever known!" And I've been known to betray myself for something greater, someone more perfect, more intelligent, more beautiful, more anything, than I am.

75

All these grand flaws I admit to. So, who am I to receive this vision? This new language? Again I ask the darkness. But Spirit will not be put off. The answer comes quickly. Who am I not to respond to this vision? Who am I to deny the calling of Spirit? The words and images keep coming like sparks suddenly released from a burning log. They persist like the hum of a Jew's harp in a master's hand. But, before I share with you my masterpiece, let me share with you another shiny pearl from the necklace of my lovely friend and spiritual healer—a necklace that you can bet charmed me, even disarmed me, so that she could work her healing energy through my thick skin down into the marrow of my bones. This one I even put on a sign and taped to my small oak desk.

DO WHAT SCARES YOU THE MOST.

Something Henry David Thoreau once said to her, I believe.

Being honest with myself and others scared me the most. To express my innermost feelings, without the distance of philosophy as a buffer, terrified me. You might think truthfulness would be a burning ambition for a poet. Or at least my best intention. But truth can live behind so many veils and in so many hidden places. There are many doors to the truth within us but the digging shovel or the battering ram will not open these doors. I have learned that most often the very doors that look and feel like devouring monsters, once opened, will reveal the most exquisite and gentle truths about ourselves. Whereas the doors that seem to offer us the greatest escape, these doors contain the very monsters we fearfully, continually, seek to avoid. Life is strange that way. You have to desire truth with your whole heart. Then you must court truth as a lover. With vulnerability and honor. With fearlessness and purity and quietness. With a tightrope balance of boldness and sensitivity. With deep trust and intimacy and commitment and hard work and perseverance. And certainly not with hands like dissecting shears. Or with a heart sticky and possessive as flypaper. Or with a mind like a steel trap. Or a mind like my own that yakky yaks all the time. Especially when it's cold out there and I'm in a warm bed and putting off the inevitable. Angelina stirs and smiles in her dreams. She sleeps in the nude. I sneak my head beneath the covers to kiss her a few lingering times.

76

She moans softly. Half-awake now she cradles my head to her heart. Ah, such womanness, such playfulness. I want to stay longer. I want to enter her. As if to find the origin of the world in the solid fact of her body. But the urgent call of Spirit will not abate. I slip from our warm bed and the circle of Angelina's arms. I tiptoe past our Divine Mother and into the kitchen. I make a cup of coffee and sit at the kitchen table. I start to write. Images flicker alive in my hands like tiny candles. They seem to have a life of their own.

Suddenly I stop.

I hear the muffled voices of fishermen passing beneath my kitchen window. Then quietness. I hear the Aegean Sea. Always I hear the sea! Like an ancient lullaby at times. At times like an angry tyrant. At times like a lover knowing my innermost thoughts. And at times like a good friend, steadfast and true.

Speaking of good friends, Eden Maldek should be here. Eden likes a good story and tells even better ones, if you know what I mean. Like Bubu, he enhances the details with a keen sense of drama and emotional exuberance. He lies a little too, I suppose. Anything to give the tale more power. Eden looks so serious and intense and philosophical most of the time. Like a man with a great mission to accomplish. Like Moses in the Old Testament. Or a fourteenth century alchemist, dabbling in the Secret Arts. And he's secretive, like a pirate. Eden has this great curiosity and fascination with the dark energies. He likes to live in the shadows, to observe and to draw power from the darkness. Living on the edge this way gives him the illusion that he's able to go beyond his own limitations. He thinks he can draw specialness from the darkness, and in this way create an image that's larger than life, in the same way you make huge frightening shadows on the walls with your hands and fingers. This allows him to maintain a certain aloofness and a feeling of invulnerability. Even his physical appearance supports this larger-than-life image—his long, dark hair, sometimes wound in a single braid behind his back; his barrel chest; the intense, almost Mongolian look in his eyes; the coiled energy around his body. I saw him the other day down by the harbor.

He came ashore from the passenger boat that stops by once a week from Athens. I'm seeing things of course. How could Eden Maldek be in Monemvasia? But for that brief moment, I swear....

Then, early the next morning, up came the sea captain and he had "Eden" with him. Jesus, he even talked like Eden. A slow, soft voice with strength, like the voice of movie actor Burt Lancaster. But this Greek "Eden" is a university student home for the holidays. His mother lives here. He seemed a bit bewildered, or amused, maybe even mystified, by the whole situation. And how like Eden!

The captain warned me the sea was dangerous that day. He said I shouldn't venture out. The day before, Angelina and I had gone with Bubu and Labés to a little village up the coast. Bubu has a friend back in Germany who keeps a sailing yacht moored for winter in the harbor of this village. Bubu wanted to make sure everything on the boat was in good order. He hired Labés and his fishing boat to take him to the village and asked us to go along. Bubu wanted to show us the ruins of a Mycenaean temple in the hills overlooking the sea near the village, and the nearby ruins of an ancient wall and doorway that had been built long before human beings understood the concept of an arch. But to go out that morning never entered my mind. And why, of all people, should the captain have chosen "Eden" as our interpreter? I'm sure he had a perfectly natural reason. And yet—and yet—.

Bottoms up! It's a mystery to me!

How the world came into being

Once there were three Divine beings. One called Man, one called Woman, and the other called Child. Man went out to put on airs. First he built a fire. He forged an arrow to penetrate the mysteries of time and overcome space. He analyzed a tree and invented the wheel. Man traveled in grand circles and wrote a book on Chance & Circumstance and called his designs to control the world "The Great Purpose." (Man feared death, he feared to be alone; but most of all Man feared the unknown.) He imagined his destiny among the stars and played very serious games with names that Child could never remember and which bored Woman to tears. Man suffered with great pride and would not give up his arrogant ways.

Soon, Woman grew weary of breathing dust and stirring the coals. After all, Woman could envision a totally different world. A world of feelings and relationships and ever-changing forms and colors. The color red she envisioned for the awakening of desire and green to herald the Earth and the coming of Child. Yellow she gave to the intense summer Sun and to the flowers that loved her gladness, and blue she gave to the sea and to the reflection in Man's eyes whenever he looked upon the world without lust or impatience or greed for power. (To edge Man onward she called her vision of a new consciousness NO MORE WAR.) Woman needed orange for balance and for the autumn leaves that delighted Child when they fell from the trees and whirled about upon the garden path; and pink she created so the mind would not freeze in abstractions. Purple she placed on the inner rim of the rainbow, and in the amethyst she wore over her heart, and in the bedroom curtains near the fireplace. (Woman was never quite sure of purple.) Then, without wavering an eye, Woman appeared in radiant white.

This mystified Child, who stared in wonder.

Child longed to be like Man in all his marvelous adventures, but Man would not speak of the great mysteries, but only repeat what he had been told with great authority. Child turned to Woman for comfort, but Woman looked too busy putting spring flowers in her hair and wishing Man would come to his senses.

Child felt utterly alone.

"I will not play these games!" cried Child. "I will not memorize names and ancient causes and I will not be deceived by appearances."

Child vowed this intention with such clarity and with such boldness that, like a dream that awakens the dreamer, or like a bird of pure light, the desire within Child's heart instantly cut through Man's circular reasoning and startled Woman from her enchanting arts.

Deep within consciousness, a leaf trembled. The wheel burst into flame and the flame into a human heart.

This is how Man and Woman saw each other for the first time.

And this is how the world came into being.

Remembrance of you

They say you were born when the earth & mountains
turned green and bright yellow,
& bees swarmed the hills to gather flowers
for their Queen,
& goats with singing throats
roamed the rocks.
The blue morning sea and sky
were one
in the moment of your awakening.
You saw the oneness of life,
& you saw the oneness
dissolve
before your eyes
into so many streams,
& the streams into an unwavering light
within you

I stopped, not knowing how to end the poem. I was sitting alone at Johan's big table, using his old manual typewriter with the Danish alphabet. It was late April and the hills on the road between Sparta and Monemvasia had turned bright yellow with tall flowering shrubs. These fragrant, bright yellow flowers reminded me of the Scotch broom growing along the freeways in Oregon. The singing goats came from that incredible evening as the sun was going down and a goat herder with his dog was herding more than a hundred goats into a canyon corral for the night. The sound of the goats in the wind at dusk in the shadows quickly darkening into night, and a starry sky with a crescent moon, held us motionless, enchanted. In the near distance, the lights of Yephra twinkled and we could hear the sea lapping the land with soft, dark, unending waves.

One morning, late in February, I had looked out over the old fortress walls of Monemvasia and gazed into the bluest sea and sky that I had ever seen. For a moment I stood still and quiet, becoming a

81

part of the blue oneness I gazed upon. I decided this sparkling azure sea could, indeed, have been the birthplace of Venus. Like the Venus I had seen in a painting by Alexander Cabanel. The Goddess, in all her soft and sensuous beauty, lies sleeping (or perhaps she dreams?) on the ocean froth. Frolicking above her in the air, little winged cherubs are blowing conch shells. I could well imagine that she must have been the most gorgeous woman Alexander Cabanel had ever painted. Probably he fell in love with her and that was the death of the artist as a normal man. For a moment, I amused myself with this thought. Then it dawned on me how much this blue Aegean sea and sky reminded me of the gemstone we found in a shop in Athens.

It was a small shop on one of the winding streets that eventually leads up to the Acropolis. Angelina and I walked into the shop by chance, or so we thought. We were looking for a fire opal to have set in silver as a wedding ring for Angie. She had combed the little jewelry shops in the Flea Market area of London, but had seen none she really liked. Here in this little shop in the Plaka we found what she wanted: a lovely and brilliant Australian fire opal in a simple silver setting. It was a beautiful ring and, no doubt, symbolic in some way of our marriage. As for myself, I seldom wear jewelry. Not even a watch. I don't care for metal things on my hands. So I was just curiously looking at the rings inside the glass case when a blue sky stone, set in a man's silver ring, caught my eye. I had never seen a stone like this before. The blue was as blue as the Aegean Sea, but with a hint of white clouds. Like the earth seen from outer space. I asked to see the ring and it was a perfect fit. As perfect as my large knuckles allowed. The proprietor of the store—a man who looked more Turkish or Middle Eastern than Greek—motioned for his daughter, who spoke good English, to answer our questions about the ring. She called the stone Larimar, and said it's found in only one place in the world—a mine recently discovered on an island in the Dominican Republic

She looked at me curiously, or so I imagined.

The woman was about my own age and had coal black hair and luminous eyes and an earthly, sensual beauty in her face. "It is a stone of free will and free joy," she said, articulating her words slowly and precisely. Her eyes glowed with an inner light, as if she were seeing into the heart of the stone. "I see this to be the Child's Stone. A stone of being who you wish to be—and doing what you wish to do—with the freedom of the child. A stone of knowing how you feel and what you want—as a child knows—instinctively."

I slipped the stone on the ring finger of my right hand and imagined myself wearing it. For me, this blue stone was the stone of the warm shallow seas and the white cloud sky. The stone of the wanderer who finds joy and never loses his way.

The woman, still looking at the ring with warm, dreamy eyes, raised one hand to her neck and pulled a thin silver chain from beneath her black wool sweater. On the chain, set in a delicate silver loop, was another blue sky stone.

"I love this stone," she said to us, almost in a whisper. "I keep it with me all the time. It is the stone of a Dreamer."

A quiver of excitement showed in her voice. Angelina squeezed my hand. We both felt honored that this woman had shown us her personal power stone. Glancing at the ring still on my finger, the woman said, "These are Dreaming stones. They carry a new message to the world."

What did she mean by that? I was afraid to ask, afraid the question would break the magical spell. Looking at the stone on my finger in that strangely warm and dreaming way, the woman said, "I feel this is your stone. Yes. The Child's Stone is your personal stone."

Perhaps she was just saying this to sell me the ring, quibbled the doubter in me. But I don't think so. She was not a woman to lie about such things. Besides, I had made up my mind to take the ring right from the beginning. I felt that the energy of the blue sky stone was closely connected to my heart. I bought the ring and Angelina took the fire opal and we walked back down the hill, both in a slightly astonished dream.

But the inspiration for the poem…?

83

The elusive chemistry, the subtle indivisibility of this remembrance, felt to me like a fleeting dream in the early morning light; like a moonbeam in the grasses or the shadow of a hand against a tree limb; like the dancing flitter of light among trees or the pattern of reflections in water or the movement of a young girl passing by a window: all these things that come and go, that you see and do not know if you really saw or not.

I wanted a good ending to my poem. Something solid, final, unshakable. To be the few notes of a melody heard faraway and not the complete song, this felt most unsettling to my mind. I was used to thinking in terms of tight, defined structures, and the routines of daily life, and concrete forms that seemed to defy the changes of time and the tides. In my belief system, I judged things right or wrong; real or not real. The undefined: all those things that you couldn't touch, and that have no continuity, belonged to the world of illusion and fantasy and to the dangerous and watery realm of Neptune. But not to the planet Earth. I could not imagine that the essence of the life force might happen randomly from day to day, here today, somewhere else tomorrow, a bit of this, a pinch of that, a little piece of sunray, a little rainbow, a dewdrop, a flower, a butterfly's wings traced against the sun. I could not believe that these things might contain any real meaning, expressed in a way that only the peripheral of my mind, the edges of my sight, the inner ear, the half-beat between my heart beats, could understand. Nor could I see that these elusory impressions and fleeting images and memories that could not be made tangible, or stuck into some rigid category, or confined in a system, or explained by a theory, or controlled by the laws of this or that: all these things that come and go, that slip past the corner of your eye, that you see and do not know if you really saw or not, contain the essence of magic and beauty and playfulness and are just as real and meaningful and alive as the life animals live or plants live or human beings live; that these things are more than just frosting and adornment and ornaments solicited by a none-too-real imagination, —or temptations that would lead me astray into sloth and indolence and false longings; but they are living strands of energy and power and essence that help to keep the mind from turning rigid and cold and going dead; and through these things that come and go, that you see and do not know if you really saw or not; that through these flights of fantasy, these delicate ribbons of light, these rainbow colors, these fleeting dreams, I might cease this ancient war with myself and bring a great opening to my heart and to my mind and to the other energy centers of my body, and create within and around myself a kind of healing spaciousness and a gentle passage that would bring me home to the truth of my being, to the wholeness of personality and self, and to my unremembered identity.

The big iron gate

I see a man in pain and a man who wants death,
and a man who asks, *"Why?"*

He turns to me in anger;
and I hear an old man talking to the stars.
"What do the stars tell you, Old Man?"

The old man mumbles under a great moustache,
"Tonight the stars are joking with me!"

And I hear the guards closing the big iron gate.

Beyond walls

To see you for just moments—
my heart turns to rage.

I'm in prison, guards at every turn.

I see you through an iron screen.
I love you beyond walls,
beyond rage and the guards.

Remember, they shot Garcia Lorca.
They tried Blake for treason.
Who escapes?

To be free

The greatest wonder in life,
and on earth, is this:
to see, to love, to be free.

Anger, greed, selfishness, pride:
all are prisons.
They limit my spirit.

Only love does not limit my spirit.

The cry

for Douglas Blazek

Love- being an essential word —
Begin this song, envelop it all.
—Carlos Drummond De Andrade

Love!
The very stones cry out,
as poets make old hats
& twist sur-
realism
into a mathematical
landscape.

Bravo,
worn out history
& women in dreams.
Bravo, the everlasting sonnet
—a corpse
on rue Saint-Lazare
where the River Seine
overflows black oil,
misery
& initiation into death.

Love!
The very stones cry out
in so many languages,
surely the stones
have retreated into the desert,

or sank into the poisonous sea;
as work horses transform
our dreams into a cellular fog,
& love turns the other way,
seeking the heart
clear of smoke and relics.

Melancholia: over-indulgence;
anger & bitterness.
Some mornings, I swear,
my soul will not bear
another day in this prison cell.

Ten times worse

Look, here I am in a Greek prison,
& workers are hammering
yet another roof over my head,
high above the walls.
I find distraction in symbols,
while my neighbor groans in his sleep.
One man worships a cross;
another man kills his mother.

Each moment is a replaceable part
in this prison;
each act a play for mercy.
We walk from one cell to the other;
we pace the concrete yard
& with nervous steps, we wear out infinity.

The world bitches without pause.
There's no end to misery!
We're prisoners of the past, the future,
of everything we know
& of all that we do not know.
We're prisoners of thought.

In stillness comes the fire

The Farm...Will I ever see the Farm?
Evergreens and Oregon rains...homemade peach ice
cream...peppermint tea and Naomi and yellow
wildflowers by the stream....
    Day and night in this prison
    I dream.
        Enough!
        Be still and flow.

        I am here,
        and truth is just *this*.

Only the earth

Christmas comes and goes,
& now it's Easter time.

Look, here comes the priest!
Aw, he's old and fat,
he looks like death warmed over.
Around him, candles burning,
chant a dozen prisoners.

The seven locked gates
he sprinkles with holy water.
Inside, we quietly celebrate
our beer and cakes,
& the sacrificial entrails
we throw to the cats.

The wind whirls ashes before my eyes,
clouds gather in the sky.
The night falls in rain.
And only the earth—
this earth that catches
& transforms my spirit—
only the earth is my resurrection.

On the work farm

A newborn calf kicks up its heels
& in the distance, across the sea,
past ancient olive trees, I gaze
upon the home of the ancient gods,
snow-capped Mt. Olympus.
A calm blue sea laps the fires
of Ithaca.

    Bravo,
there's only ONE truck to unload!
We're spitting dust, stacking
bales of hay high into the barn
—a barn made of concrete,
encircled by guards in towers
& loaded guns; hills,
bright with golden wheat,
rippling to the water's edge.

    2
I drag my body to an apple tree
& wipe the sun from my forehead.
Is this the Tree of Life,
of Knowledge, of Good and Evil?
This isn't the tree of my dreams;
this isn't the farm I had in mind!

"Let's go! Let's go!"
barks an impatient guard.
I dig a circle around the tree;
only three thousand more to go....

Chopping corn

War!

We grab our choppers and run.
"Inside, inside!" the two-striper shouts.
They lock all doors; confiscate radios.
The guards wait: ON ALERT.

A storm blows in off the sea.
Even the elements agree:
Clear the air! Revolution is here!

        2
Cyprus, her cities bombed
by Turkish fighters,
portends doom for the Greek junta;
and rumors, faster than war planes,
fly inside these prison walls.
In Athens, the army falls
to the people in the streets;
& the old Prime Minister
they recall.

THIS IS OUR CHANCE.
THE KING WILL RETURN AND SET US FREE.
(FOR SURE!)

        3
The days come and go.
We go back
To chopping corn.

        4
Black crows in a wheat field,
White moon in a blue sky.
On the hill, a circle of goats;
& on the sea a blazing sun.

"Dear Amur," her letter begins

I shake my head in amazement. Naomi has such a strange sense of humor. Just before I left America, we had a long talk together, one of the few times we've ever spoken to each other without pretending we were talking about something else. She told me about a dream she had. In her dream she and I—only she called me Amur—were living with our people in a tribe on the edge of some middle-Eastern desert. We were living as husband and wife and had a small son and another child on the way. I tended animals and worked with her father. We were so much in love with each other, she told me. Our minds and feelings were so closely connected, they seemed to be one, and although I was a quiet man and spoke little, she seemed to always know what I was thinking in my heart. Naomi saw the second child being born but something went wrong, there was some difficulty, and she felt all this pain in her body, and suddenly she was no longer in her body.

She saw me walking in the desert, alone, and weeping.

She had never seen me weep before. I seemed to be looking for something. "Amur, my beloved," she called, "why are you so sad? What are you seeking?"

As if I could hear her voice, I answered: "Naomi is gone."

We sat for a long time in silence and she watched me, not fully understanding my meaning. Suddenly I spoke again. Without taking my eyes from the desert, I said: "I come seeking God. I come to the desert to call upon this God of Our Fathers. This God was the breath between Amur and Naomi. Only she understood Amur. Only she could see into his heart. Now I come seeking HIM."

"Amur, Amur, my beloved," she murmured and reached out to touch me with her hands; her small, warm hands that I had loved so well. "Do not seek Our God in this barren land, my beloved!" she cried. "Look inside to your heart. There, in your heart, God is, even as I am." I swiftly lifted my eyes from the ground, as if hearing a sudden sound in the still desert air.

Aspirations of a poet
or,
a minor urge to explain myself

Heaven's own, ringed servants
& dust in his fiery hair,
& his spirit wrapped in blue

At first, the poet bends the world to his desire. He distorts appearances. The poet nourishes upon his great emptiness. Greed swells his eyes and clutters his bowels. Envy obscures his vision. To hurry, forces him to invent. He loses touch, he stalls and overexposes himself. He plays the Fool, the Beast, the Chosen One. (The ego is a master of disguises, have you not noticed? And I use the male pronoun only for convenience. Man, woman, child: we're all in the same leaky boat.) The poet reminds us how he sees the world in a "special way." (Through his nose, up against the mirror.) He's terribly sensitive, this poet, and you're on thin ice. He craves attention. He's jealous of power and always stares into the light, which causes him to squint perpetually. His words possess secret intimations—clues to his astral whereabouts. (He's usually in the bedroom, second only to God, and out on a limb.) Life turns on him at every corner. He suffers out of neglect and false pride. (It is not yet his time). But, here and there, the great poet catches with his verses a single, shining moment, a glimmer of truth and his individuality, the oneness of all life, the continuous stream of creativity that flows through each of us. He's horrified, delighted, ecstatic. Which is real—this world of appearances, or the mind? And is there a difference? And how do we know? (How do we know anything?) How will the poet escape self-deception? *What he is, is what he sees.*

*****

To speak directly to your heart (there's only one way), I must write from the heart. When the words come through the heart, try as I may, I cannot force the image. I start out to say, "I love you," and end up in a cosmological fire. One day, at Nafplion, I found a tiny, bright yellow flower in the prison yard. How this tiny flower escaped from being crushed by all the men walking back and forth, I know not. But there it was.

I've always been somewhat passive when it came to "choosing" events that ultimately shaped the current of my life, believing, like Don Quixote before the Windmills, that Fortune directs my Destiny better than I ever will. So sometimes I find myself in the oddest places. What I thought to be Windmills, turns out to be Giants; and these Giants wear uniforms with a dull metallic eye over their foreheads, so that I won't be deceived.

What would I be doing if not in this Greek prison?

Is this karma or destiny? Or just a twist in the stream?

Often I've wondered how San Juan de la Cruz could have written such cheerful and luminous songs of the Spirit while imprisoned in a castle dungeon.

My question seems meaningless.

I am here.

In other words, *Am I not the stream?*

*****

Transformations,
diabolical urges &
divine inspiration

As a man and a poet, I would tell you the truth and nothing but the truth. I would show you my deep, heartbeating love for the mystery, the beauty, the stillness, the wonder, the vibrancy, believing this to be my purpose and the purpose of all poetry. But I live as if truth is something Out There. Something that fits all, like a pair of stretch socks. Something that can be put into words and theories like the speed of light, or the cure for the common cold, or the number of angels on the petal of a medieval rose. I live in the past, in ancient imprints—memories that limit and tighten my mind like a surgical ecraseur; or like the Chinese cloth bindings that were once used on the feet of female babies, in order to keep their feet small.

98

There are moments...there are moments.

But fear gets in my way.

"Come!" I would say to truth. I would face my fears. I would drop all my pretenses. But they go too deep, too close, to my heart. Deeper than my meditations; deeper than my realizations. I still love the drama more than stillness. I love the excitement more than silence. Even enlightenment is something you do, something you achieve. Even Now is something you experience and hold onto in your mind. Something you control. I live in fear, but I will not acknowledge this. That would be unmanly. I need safety, but that does not fit into my image of a poet. Within me abides a great power: the power of tenderness and kindness and honesty, and the power of letting others be. But I will not acknowledge this. This power lies in wait behind the images that I fear so greatly. The images of separateness and death, pain and loss. I feel caught in a drama and I do not recognize the actor I play. I see the dreaming of the world but do not know the dreamer.

*****

Angelina and I are walking together by a stream in a quiet wood. We're holding hands and laughing. Suddenly, a deer appears before us. A lovely, magical deer. This magical deer will answer any question we desire to ask. We must ask quickly, without a moment's hesitation. I know exactly what I want to know. "What is the meaning of my life?" Instantly there appear before me two open hands, large hands like my own, filled with ashes.

I wake up. I'm in my bed in a Greek prison. I feel alive, happy. The handful of ashes does not sadden me. They do not intimate my death or loss or annihilation. I understand this image represents a process of purification, of cleansing; the refinement of gross experience. Like Rumi, I have entered the divine fire. Like Ramprasad, I can say: "I have offered my gift." I have harvested the wisdom of my human experience. I have increased my knowledge (and the knowledge of all beings) and now I'm going home.

Kassandra, Greece, 1974

99

The days come and go

In the orchards, Greek prisoners gather shiny red apples into big piles and haul them off to feed the pigs. We stuff our pockets full as we pass the apple trees on our way to the cornfields, the guards turning their heads and pretending not to see. It's October, the days clear and warm with mellow sunlight. After we harvest the corn—the scrawniest, wormiest bunch of ears I've ever seen—the prison cows munch their way haphazardly through the rows. We follow the cows with our choppers, knocking over the dead stalks and piling them into huge stacks and then burning the fields. The good ears we find, we roast in the burning coals. Coming back inside each day, we plunder the pear trees growing near our path, robbing them of their low-hanging fruit as the guards swear and shout at us that these pears are no good. One day, I realize that the two black-and-white storks have gone. Each spring they return to the farm, to mate in a large nest they built on the roof of the supply barn. I smile, remembering their graceful flights across the valley.

The nights turn cold. A small wood burner is all we have for heat in the room, and before winter is out, we won't be able to go near the damn thing, it'll be smoking so badly. The guards allow us one sack of firewood each day and an armful of corn cobs for kindling. Last winter, a big snow fell on Kassandra, a peninsula on the Aegean Sea, not far from Thessaloniki in the northern district of Macedonia. It got so cold on the work farm that the foreigners broke up their bed boards and threw the pieces into the stove, along with bars of olive oil prison soap, books, anything that would burn. It's forbidden to cook on the wood stove. But, as soon as the guards lock the doors in the evening, we cook everything from brown rice, to Italian spaghetti with savory sauce, to English puddings.

On Thanksgiving, the American consul in Thessaloniki shows up with a roasted turkey and stuffing, gravy, cranberry sauce, pumpkin pie. There are six of us Americans at Kassandra. I share turkey and a piece of pie with Alex Demianenko, who was born in Montreal, just a few weeks after his parents arrived in Canada from the Ukraine during the war years. Still, it seems a bit strange, eating Thanksgiving dinner in a room with "foreigners."

100

We pick olives in the crisp, early mornings of November and in the drizzling December rains, and we snack on wild blackberries growing in the hills among the oldest olive trees near the sea. One guard tries to warn us that these berries are poisonous. (Even as he's telling us this, in the distance we see the gun guard stuffing berries into his mouth.) *Dhembirazi,* we go to great lengths to smuggle the poison blackberries inside so that we can eat them with yogurt or milk.

The early morning sky never ceases to amaze me with its breathtaking changes, as the sun breaks over the curtain of clouds above the valley. On a clear day, I can even catch a glimpse of Mt. Olympus—that old snow-capped rascal—just across the sea. We take a short break from picking olives and I gaze without pity or regret upon this blue Aegean Sea, knowing I shall probably never see this beautiful land again. Already this country seems like a memory to me.

The whole room turns to light

Alex Demianenko quietly paints a picture of a prisoner in his stonewall cell, as the prisoner meditates on a book. A shaft of light streams through the bars of the prisoner's small window. He could almost be a monk in some monastery cell. As Demianenko quietly paints, Keith Guellow writes a letter to his friends in Amsterdam. Across from us, on the other side of the room, four men gamble with cards—handmade cards that the ever-watchful guards missed in their last search. The guards also missed the camera smuggled in by Whitmore, when his sister came to visit him. (That's me in the center, wearing a tattered straw hat, next to Australian Mike, and the old fellow from Pakistan.) At the moment, I'm sitting cross-legged on my bed. A few minutes ago I took a shower. A rare shower, you can bet, because the only water we have is so incredibly cold. Yet my body feels warm, comfortable, quiet. All day I've been pondering the words of the Russian writer Solzhenitsyn in *Gulag Archipelago*. "Every human being has a point of view—Every human being is the Center of the Universe."

Suddenly, my thoughts stop.

Just like that.

The whole room becomes instantly, totally luminous. Not like other nights, when I've experienced the room as a gradual, brightening glow. Tonight it's like an explosion or a cosmic dance. It's like nothing I've ever known before. It's like the heavens opened up, if you can imagine that. The brightness fills the whole room, everyone and everything, and then everyone and everything seems translucent, everything appears radiant, clear, and I am filled with this tremendous, superloving energy, this unlimited joy. Everything around me contains this energy. I am not in a trance. My mind has not gone blank. Yet the few thoughts that come and go seem like strands or wisps of thin clouds across an empty sky. How long this illumination lasts, I do not know. A moment. Ten minutes. Perhaps twenty. The light seems to go on and on and I have no sense of time or fatigue or incompleteness. I feel so alive and joyful, humming with love.

That night of stars

Let me remember THAT NIGHT
OF STARS over the Aegean Sea,
& the Scorpions (those awful
Scorpions!) that slept
Beneath the rocks in our garden,
& let me remember (this one
      time only)
Before we are swept away into
Eternity after eternity,
Just how your arms enCircled me,
& the air was quiet THAT NIGHT
OF STARS over the Aegean Sea

Total fire, at last

1975-1981

§

*I think marriage is the hottest furnace of the
spirit today.*
—Leonard Cohen

§

*Remember,
I was here, and you were here,
and together we made a world.*
—David Whyte
"The Poet As Husband"

Total fire

I enter the sweet passage to your womb
and merge with the flow of your blood.
I come home to your love,
and my birth is remembered in the singing
of your nerves.

I enter the dark passage to your womb
and the way feels deep and unknown.
I have no protection but your love,
and the joyous cry of your heart.

I enter the sacred passage to your womb
and leave all thoughts behind.
I know only your love,
and love's mercy ever-shining in your eyes.

I enter the burning passage to your womb
and my ashes mingle with your ashes.
I live in your love,
and I shall love you forever and forever.

Portland, Oregon
October 1975

All those years

From *This Passing World / Journey from a Greek Prison*

Naomi sipped her lukewarm coffee. A half-smoked cigarette lay burning in the ashtray. Earlier, she had turned on the radio to her favorite country music station, but now she hardly hears the words to the song. Willie Nelson singing about blue eyes crying in the rain. Did she know anyone with blue eyes? Oh, yes, Melina Foster. She and Melina didn't get along very well. Naomi had tried to be friends with her. A best friend, like a sister. But they never did anything together. Never went anywhere together. Not even to a movie. Melina would call when she wanted help with her hair. It was always when she needed something. Never just to chit-chat. Never just to be friends. Melina reminded Naomi of her mother. They were both wiry, sensitive, nervy women with sharp edges. They both had a flair for drama. Her mother getting into a drunken rage at Clyde and throwing the dishes across the room and smashing them. Not the good ones of course. The good dishes she kept in the china cabinet. It had been so different with her real dad. Her real dad died when she was eight. They were living in Idaho then. He got caught out in his truck in a blizzard. He tried to keep warm using the truck heater. They say he died of carbon monoxide.

Her real dad had been a preacher. His name was Virgil. He had a kind heart and played the guitar. She'd sit on his knees and he'd sing to her "You Are My Sunshine." He'd tell her stories. He wrote poetry too. They had been best buddies until he died. She felt betrayed. She felt angry at him for leaving her. Her mother had tried to explain that it wasn't her fault he had died, but no matter what her mother told her, she still felt guilty, as if she had done something wrong. As if he went away because of her. The child inside her clutched this feeling tightly to her heart, as if, somehow, if she carried this feeling around long enough, her dad would come back and everything would be all right again.

But things only got worse. She hated her step-dad. He was not at all like her real dad. Clyde worked hard, long hours at his job and he drank a lot. When he drank, he and mom almost always got into a fight. Clyde had his own construction company, but no social skills. He

108

built restaurants for a fast food franchise. They would send him to Colorado for two years. Then to Georgia. Then to California. Her family was always moving. Clyde made good money, but he had a tight-fisted heart. He acted as if he was doing the kids a big favor, taking care of them.

Her mom had been sixteen when she married Virgil. She was ignorant. She didn't know anything. But Naomi remembered only good things about Virgil. Even if she couldn't believe in his God. There had been other men in her mom's life, after Virgil's death. They drove motorcycles and didn't have jobs. Here, Norma had five kids. What was she thinking?

Then there was Jules. Jules seemed safe at first and kind-hearted. He befriended her mom and for a brief time they were lovers. But for some reason, Jules had to go out of town and that's when her mom met Clyde. Later, Jules came back to visit them, pretending to be an old friend.

Naomi was fourteen then. For some reason, Jules felt Norma had betrayed him. Naomi didn't understand his reasons at the time. All she knew was that one night, when her mom and Clyde were out for the evening, Jules came to her room. Jules warned her not to tell anyone about what happened between them that night. Naomi kept quiet. She never spoke of this to her mom, ever. She felt sure than Norma would blame her. Jules came to her room many times after that first night. He taught her ways of pleasing a man. She liked Jules. He paid attention to her. He didn't treat her like a stupid teenager. At times, the idea of having sex with her mother's old boyfriend had excited her. At other times, she felt guilty and scared. When Jules left for California, he told her how she could get in touch with him, if ever she needed help. She never told anyone about Jules, not even Marcus. The whole thing left her feeling weird. Men didn't feel safe anymore. No matter how much you loved them, they betrayed you, they used you, they left you.

*****

Marcus had helped her out of a jam. He gave her a job in the pizza place he was managing in Atlanta and he never said anything out of line to her. He thought she was a virgin when they met. That was almost eight years ago. The summer of '66. Slowly, those old feelings of trust and friendship she had felt with her real dad began to re-surface. She knew she could trust Marcus. He wouldn't hurt her. They shared a real bond of love and friendship. She knew, however, that it had been the wrong thing for her to marry him. She didn't really want to, but she couldn't come up with any real reason not to. After all, they were living together. He certainly loved her. What else do you do?

At least Marcus wasn't an alcoholic. He would never hit her and he wouldn't cheat on her. He was a good provider and he felt a deep responsibility to their marriage, after his first two failures. But... and this next thought terrified her... she felt no passion between them. What romance she had felt in the beginning, even that was gone now. There was just a feeling of deadness there. Even the little, extra things that she used to do, like hanging stockings at Christmas, she stopped. Marcus didn't know what to do. He would never ask for help or go to a marriage counselor. Our problems are our private business, he said. She knew he knew about her feelings for David. She had wanted to go with David and Melina Foster to the Vortex rock festival at McIver State Park. This was the famous rock festival sponsored by the State of Oregon in order to diffuse the potential street violence they feared might erupt in Portland between war protesters and the national convention of the American Legion. Governor Tom McCall had officially ordered the state police to stay out of the park during the three festival days. She pleaded with Marcus to let her go, but he wouldn't budge. He had no desire to go and he didn't want her there. He knew her real reason for going was not to smoke pot and mud wrestle or walk around naked in front of thirty thousand people or drop acid and dance all night inside a womb-like circus tent to a rock group playing "Love Is Just A Kiss Away." She wanted to go because of David. She wanted to be near him in the wild uncertainty of what might happen at that festival. And who knows what might have happened between them... inside that womb-like tent? But Marcus didn't want to deal with her feelings for David. Just like he didn't want to deal with the deadness in their marriage. He would agree to talk about it later. Later

110

would come, and nothing would be said. This happened again and again. He believed that if you just didn't talk about a problem, somehow it would go away. Or fix itself. But it wasn't going away. David was going away. But not the problem. God, David had said they might even stay in Europe.

She left the kitchen and walked into her bedroom. She started to make the bed and then remembered she was alone in the house. Marcus was working overtime this Saturday till noon. Such an awful job, welding. It hurt his back, his eyes. She would be glad when he found another job. The bed was unmade. The house was unmade. Her whole fucking life was unmade. She thought of painting the outside of their house green. From the road it would blend right in with the grove of pine trees. Maybe then she would feel safe. The world would just pass her by. She longed for a child. A female child. A friend, a sister. Years of taking fertility pills hadn't helped. Marcus certainly wasn't to blame. Something was always wrong with her system. First her mucus was hostile to his sperm. And then…

Now they were talking about adopting a baby.

She lay down on the bed. She still had her nightgown on, the blue one Marcus had given her for Christmas two years ago.

Her thoughts drifted to David. She felt a sudden panic. What if he should stay in Europe? This idea terrified her. She wanted to be near him, even if he was married to Angie. That would be okay. She smiled, thinking of the last time they were together. The four of them were taking a Sunday drive along the Columbia River Gorge. They were all riding in the front seat of Marcus' old pick-up. She and David were sitting in the middle, their legs pressing together, ever so tightly. It felt so intense she thought for sure EVERYONE knew. She stared straight ahead, afraid of looking at him.

"How can you hide something THAT BIG?" she wanted to tease. Suddenly, her whole body got hot. She lifted her nightgown and pushed down her panties before they melted. She thought of David as she closed her eyes. She thought of the times he would make love to her while she slept peacefully in his arms. He would touch her so very lightly and carefully with his finger until the moisture came, then he would slowly enter her, so as not to fully awaken her. The next morning she would linger in bed, wondering. Had she only dreamed he had come? Touching herself, she would find his seed inside her. She prayed they would make a baby together.

*****

A postcard from Paris arrived and a card from Rome. Then a card from someplace in Greece called Monemvasia. The card had a picture of a little fishing village on the Aegean Sea. With a pen, David had circled a red-tiled house near the harbor. On the message side of the card he wrote that he and Angie had rented this house from an old sea captain and his wife. Naomi studied the card, thinking of him and thinking of his modesty and those ragged cut-offs he wore sometimes and no underwear and she was about to go up the walls, that bastard.

Months passed and summer came again. She and Marcus sold their house in Portland and bought a house and five acres in the country. They put their names on a list at an adoption agency.

Then came the telegram from Angie.

David had been arrested for growing marijuana plants.

To be in jail in a foreign country—Naomi's imagination filled with dreadful images of what it must be like. She knew about the military *junta* in Greece. She knew the ruler of Greece was a petty tyrant. David had written to them about how the police had thrown some German guy in jail for playing a forbidden song. What would they do to someone for growing ten marijuana plants? The court wouldn't even let David post bail. Angie said the judge was afraid David might skip the country. "Of course he would skip the country!" Marcus said. Marcus talked about going to Greece and breaking David out of prison. "If necessary," he said. What was he doing now? Naomi wondered. She thought about his last visit. Just before taking off for Europe, he and Angelina had gone to a party a stone's throw from her house. David had taken a break from the party and walked over to say hello to Marcus. Naomi had answered the door; she was half-asleep.

112

"I was napping," she said.

Marcus wasn't home. David quickly walked back to the party.

A few days later, David stopped by to drop off some financial papers. Marcus was at work. Naomi poured David a cup of coffee. They got to talking. She told him that when he knocked on her door that evening he woke her from a dream. In her dream, they were about to make love in the back seat of a car. Then Marcus showed up in her dream and interrupted them. This happened all the time in her dreams she said.

David didn't know how to take this news. So he asked her about that night in San Francisco. No, his feelings had not lied. She had wanted him just as much as he had wanted her. Naomi asked him about the night he and Marcus got so smashed and drank everything in the house and then swore she had hidden the last joint and wouldn't tell them where. She had to drive David home in his VW with Marcus following them. David had put his head in her lap and wouldn't leave her alone and he wanted to kiss her *there*. Naomi couldn't say the word. She blushed even as she told him this much.

Oh, yes, David remembered that night quite well.

He remembered the other nights, too, the nights he was stoned and tried to touch her. Naomi studied him, but said nothing more. For her, this new information changed everything. All those years she thought he was just between women when he made passes at her. She never dreamed, even when she lay in her bed almost unable to breathe, her body so hot thinking of him, that David could really desire her. She allowed herself now to imagine David wanting her. He wanted her so much he couldn't keep his hands off her and she loved every moment. She wanted him in the mornings before crawling out of bed to go to work at the bank, and she wanted him at lunchtime in her car at the Mary S. Young State Park (if she thought no one would see them). Even with other cars in the parking lot, his large hands would slip under her dress and inside her panties and she would get so damn wet with excitement. He would teasingly lick the sticky wetness from his fingers as she watched and, looking into her eyes, he would smile so sweetly and tell her he loved her.

"Strawberries," she said, touching his lips with her fingers. "Your kisses taste like strawberries. Like ripe strawberries in the sun." She saw that her words pleased him. That made her happy.

All those years she had thought he was too romantic, impractical, a dreamer. How could any woman live with him? He was too idealistic. Don Quixote dashing here and there with a sword in his pants and a rose between his teeth. All those years wanting him. Maybe prison would change him. Maybe he wouldn't want her anymore. Thank God she was pregnant. That would give her at least another nine months to keep her feelings out of sight. When Angelina flew back from Denmark over the Christmas holidays and talked so proudly about their free style of living in Copenhagen, and all that stuff about free love, and then went off with Eden Maldek, Naomi felt all kinds of weird feelings. How could Angelina do that? David was still in Greece in jail.

And then came the miscarriage; her second one.

Rushing to the Emergency at three in the morning. All that blood and disappointment and loss. To lose the baby really hurt. It scared Naomi, too. She knew now that she had to do something about her marriage. She couldn't stay much longer. No matter what. But what would she do? What would David do? What if he stayed over in Europe? The thought of not being with him felt like a dead weight in the middle of her heart.

They had such a big house. David and Angie could live with them. They could have the downstairs bedroom next to the kitchen. David could put in a vegetable garden and he could dig out the blackberry vines that were taking over the grove of pine trees in the front yard. Naomi wanted to look at him now. She could see his face so close to hers, but his kisses felt so delicious and warm and kind on her skin that she couldn't keep her eyes open. As she lay in bed with him for the first time, her heart pounding and her hands covering her vagina, ashamed that he would find her ugly, he gently took her small hands into his large ones, calling her beautiful and beloved and kissing her with his soft, sensual lips. His kisses lingered on her crushed mouth and on her throat and nipples as he searched out secret places. Places never kissed before. Places that caused her to burn with both shame and excitement. She almost giggled. He had such soft animal noises as he hovered over her. She had never felt so looked at. Or so appreciated. She felt like some strange flower. She pictured him a hummingbird, the delicate tip of his tongue darting inside her, tasting her, sucking her, as if her whole body were nectar. She shivered suddenly. She wanted to speak but couldn't. She wanted him inside her. Now. Oh, please. She reached out instinctively. She found him and wouldn't let go. Later, she expected him to turn away from her and fall asleep. Or go make tea. Or read the morning paper. But he surprised her. He didn't leave. Instead, he wanted to talk, he wanted to hold her, he wanted to kiss her.

"I eat crackers in bed," she told him.

"So?" he said.

"And I wear socks in the winter time."

By now he suspected she was teasing him. (Although she did have awfully cold feet.)

"My boobs are too small," she protested.

"But that's not true!" David assured her. He meant it. Naomi had lovely, exquisite breasts. He was astonished at her admiration for bigness.

"And my legs are funny. You said so yourself."

"Aw, I was only teasing you, Naomi. I know how sensitive you are." But did he really?

Being away in Greece, David would have no idea how much things had changed in her marriage. Now, she almost never undressed with Marcus in the same room. She even went into the closet, closing the door, to change her clothes. She hated wearing a bra, but she never went outside the house without one. She knew Marcus wouldn't approve. Marcus even thought she was frigid.

"The space between us feels like home," she murmured.

David smiled knowingly. "Your body is my home."

"More," she whispered in his ear. "Oh, please, please."

This time she didn't cover herself.

Thinking of you

I am without words
but these in my heart
that come and go,
without elegance or
arrangement, and
leave me as I am,
thinking of you.
Where do I stop
and begin again?
There are poets who
seem to know pre-
cisely the moment
and what to say.
I am alone,
thinking of you,
and I have a sore back
your hands could heal,
and I could tell you
how the sun came up
over the hills and through
the kitchen window
this morning,
as I stood making coffee,
and, thinking of you,
I would not pretend
or even try to be
a poet.
I would be as I am,
thinking of you.

Just like that, I am born

A thousand times a day
I give you up. And
a thousand and one times
you come back.

I cannot explain myself:
who I am, how I come
and go, why I love you.

Does the wind apologize
to the scientist on the street,
and does the heart stop its beat
in order that we may understand
the universe?

Just like that, I am silent.

Surrendering

He undressed as she waited in the candlelight
of the bath,
and the hot, very hot water
steamed up the length of his body
to his face,
as she eased him into the tub,
lovingly,
with her hands.
They spoke of how she looked
with her breasts
naked and her long dark hair braided
into thin braids
over her forehead,
and her almond eyes.
(He loved her eyes!)
He wondered if she were Asian,
perhaps Tibetan,
or Native American,
as her hands gently swam
and caressed his legs, his chest
and genitals,
healing the tenseness in his mind,
savoring his male body.
Afterwards,
he built a warm fire
with spruce and apple and cherry woods.
They smoked grass
and he drank a cup of tea.
They talked of the Jedediah Smith River
and the redwoods and shamrocks,
the rope bridge
and wading across the river.

He lay with his head in her lap.
She gave him her breasts
and for a long time
he lay there,
tender as a child,
her fingers stroking his head,
and her voice, gentle
as the rain outside melting the last snow,
drifting him in her arms.
In bed,
he kissed her over and over in adoration,
his kisses like butterfly wings on fire,
and she, wet
and longing for him to enter her,
her whole body the material
and soul of his own,
each whisper on his lips
rippling through the lines and breath
of her mind
into an ecstasy, a surrendering,
into a cry.
Exhausted, motion-
less,
hardly breathing,
they lay in each other's arms.
"It's still raining," she whispered.
She pulled the covers up
and they slept.

Thoughts on a river

As day turns to night,
as our journey takes a bad
turn,
What went wrong?
Who's to blame?
we ask each other,
as we both watch
the sun
slowly
sink
behind the giant redwood trees
around us,
& I listen to the river,
flowing.
What went wrong?

The gathering storm

It happened so quickly and woke you
with a start,
the wind rushing
through the window
you had opened to cool our bedroom
and clear your head
from the talk we had in the night,
the wind slamming the door shut
and whirling the curtains across the mirror
you had danced in naked, as I watched:
a woman in her early thirties,
slender as a flame,
beautiful as the earth,
reclaiming the young girl she had lost
so long ago
to a thief, a liar,
your mother's one-time lover.

*****

I calmed you back to sleep,
stroking your head,
but I lay awake for hours thinking of our home
and listening to the wind howling.
(It blew out lights and downed power lines,
I heard the next day.)
And when I slept, I slept only between dreams
of catastrophic events
and myself alone on a strange, alien planet.

*****

Waking for the last time,
before the alarm,
I wondered to myself if perhaps this house
—our house—
was the only house in the storm?

Getting in touch with your psychic energy

We got into a fight before we left the house to go to Mala's weekend retreat at the coast. Something about Naomi's driver's license. She had misplaced her driver's license. Naomi would come into the house, toss her car keys wherever. How many times had I helped her find her keys?!? Being a reasonable man, I suggested that she put them in one place every time. A simple solution.

Not.

What she did with HER keys, HER driver's license, HER lungs—was HER BUSINESS. Not mine. Okay?

Okay.

We had been to one of Mala's retreats before, in Eugene, where she had lived with her partner, Swami Aniruddha. Both Mala and Aniruddha were sannyasins who had recently returned from the Rajneesh Ashram in Poona, India. Like my friend Aditi, they always wore a shade of orange or burgundy—at least, they did before the Ranch closed and the rules changed; and, like Aditi, they each wore a mala on a burgundy cord with a small picture of Bhagwan, like in high school when you would wear your sweetheart's class ring on a chain around your neck.

We first met Mala when she came up to Portland for a visit. Eden Maldek had urged us to go and get an "energy reading" from her. Eden had been really impressed with her psychic abilities. So was I, after the reading. It was Eden who encouraged us to go to her workshop in Eugene. I had never been to a confrontational style workshop before. I had no idea what to expect when, out of the blue, a woman started screaming. I had seen some weird shit before, and the next two days was just more weird shit. All this emotional stuff flying around the room. I immediately went into survival mode. Watch out. Stay calm. Find out what's going on. Even sitting in the center of the group, in the "hot seat," with Charlie yelling that I was "pussy whipped," I did nothing. I sat there, calm and reasonable. Thinking, I suppose, that's what I needed to do: stay calm and reasonable in the flurry of these jackals screaming for blood. Mala seemed resigned that I might never break free of my protective shell. I had no idea at the time what she meant.

Later, Mala offered a free weekend introductory workshop to a series of psychic classes she planned to teach. "Getting In Touch With Your Psychic Energy," she called it. I decided to drive down to Eugene and take the introductory class. During that weekend, Mala taught us how to feel another person's aura. How to actually touch and feel with our hands the other person's aura. There's no "how," you just do it, I discovered. With your open hands outstretched, you walk slowly, carefully, up to the other person with this intention in mind until you begin to touch their energy field. You can trace the outer dimensions of this field, where it's most intense, where it drops off, where it stops. We do it quite naturally all the time, most of us, we just get distracted by our thoughts and the internal drama that's always going on in our minds. Because of the long drive to Eugene, however—a hundred miles each way—and this would be twice a week and sometimes on weekends—I decided not to take Mala's classes. Instead, Naomi would take the classes. At the time, Naomi had stopped doing her day care and she had both the time and the interest. Charlie, Eden's friend, also wanted to take the classes. So we agreed that I would take care of Scotty, Naomi's adopted child from a previous marriage, and she and Charlie would drive down together and share gas expenses. Naomi would have to do all the driving, though, because Charlie was blind.

Meanwhile, Eden decided to go to India. He had inherited some money from his grandmother and wanted to visit the Rajneesh Ashram in Poona. So he quit his job, gave up his apartment, and made travel preparations. During this time I told him it was O.K. to use our address as a mail delivery. Things went fine until his passport got forwarded by mistake to his wife Molly, in West Virginia.

When Eden first came out to Portland from West Virginia in the late 1960s (this was before I got married and went to Greece), he showed up with Molly, who had left her husband. Molly wanted to live at the coast. She and Eden moved to Lincoln City. Then Anna Sylvan and Brian McCarty drove down to visit Molly. Anna and Brian were lovers at the time. They were living together in Portland and somehow they had met Molly.

Eden fell in love with Anna.

Anna split with Brian, and Eden left Molly in Lincoln City where she lived alone by the ocean. Eden and Anna found a place together in Portland. Then Anna got pregnant with Monica. Monica was born and for years thereafter, Anna had an on-again, off-again, romantic relationship with Eden. Anna never got married.

Molly seemed a bit scatter-brained. Spacey, I guess you'd call it. But everybody loved her. Not an unkind bone in her. A tall, thin, plain looking woman with a sweet face and dark, bodiless hair, and smallish breasts and long legs—she moved like a fish and she loved the ocean. "I don't want to grow old having never lived by the ocean," she once told us, when Melina and I were at the coast visiting her and Eden.

Molly lived at the coast for a couple of years before moving back to West Virginia. While in Greece, in prison, I got a letter from her. She knew Greek. In fact, she taught high school Latin.

Right around the time Naomi and I got married, Eden took a trip back to West Virginia. He and Molly took off to Texas and got married. I just shook my head when I heard this news. Molly had such a nonchalant attitude about life, especially about money and material things and practical matters, that anyone could have predicted she would soon drive Eden out of his tight-fisted, saturnine mind. Did he think she had changed? Was he running scared, feeling the pressure of time? I had no idea. Looking back, I think he wanted redemption, but I didn't understand this at the time.

Molly came back to Portland with Eden. This lasted about three months. Eden threw her out on the street. Over money matters, I think. She did this, she did that. For Christ sake, Eden, what did you expect? I thought to myself. How long have you known Molly? You knew she was this way. But I didn't say anything.

Molly disappeared back to West Virginia.

But she never got a divorce from Eden.

And now she had Eden's passport. Or she did have it. She told Eden

124

she had sold it. Eden got hopping mad. He was ready to report her to the FBI when his passport finally arrived in the mail.

Meanwhile, he and Naomi decided to get to know each other. Eden didn't really know Naomi. He had never even said much to her. They decided to have coffee together, have lunch, drink a little wine, talk about Mala's psychic classes. Well, I had been around the block once with Eden Maldek. The minute I heard about Molly and the passport, I saw trouble ahead. Knowing Eden's history and knowing how vulnerable things felt between Naomi and me at the time, and how restless and inexperienced Naomi felt with men—I knew exactly what would happen. I really did. I watched the curtain go up and I watched it come down. The only thing that surprised me, the only thing I couldn't predict, was how much pain I would go through.

§

from Going into the darkness / Tales of past times
(an unpublished novel)

Dancing in the fire

I wanted to follow you down
that night, down passages
of soft,
forgotten skies,
down romantic nights of youth,
nights sparkling with fireflies;
and long, long days of growing up
in the South
of pale yellow honeysuckles
by the side of a red clay dirt road,
of green apple trees
in watermelon fields and ripe strawberries;
and wild, black, bittersweet cherries
I tasted each summer, *just to see.*
I wanted to remember you absolutely.
I wanted to dance you, that night,
I wanted to be you;
I wanted to hear the oceanic cry,
the roar-hum that breaks my heart
with each broken wave,
dancing, dancing,
in each joyous awakening
of your body.

I looked around the room for Sandy. We had danced together the night before, the first night of the Gearhart retreat, danced to Donna Summers' "On the Radio."

"Would you mind, sir, coming down to earth and repeating that question?"

"A dance?" I said. "Would you join me in a dance?"

"Oh, God," she signed. "I thought you'd never ask."

Sandy kept teasing me, saying outrageously coy lines in this Southern

Belle accent that got my own Southern blood up and crowing like a rooster. We were just a boy and a girl, having fun.

I enjoyed the flirtation with Sandy. But what I really wanted to do—I really wanted to dance with Naomi.

It was the only time I felt close to her the whole weekend. "I love the way you love me," Donna sang and whispered and moaned. "Our love will last forever," and, as I danced with Naomi, I wanted to believe the words to the song. I wanted to believe, like the bravado actor John Wayne battling his last battle with cancer: I can whip this thing.

Only Mala and Aniruddha out-danced us. You could actually see the electricity flashing from Mala as she danced. I had never seen such a dancer. Beautiful, willowy, graceful, Mala danced and I saw bursts of light energy around her. It was like watching a Fourth of July celebration inside a tent.

The next morning, Sandy and I ran into each other in the kitchen.

"Hey," she said, "you can stay out of my dreams! You were in my dreams last night."

She's still teasing me, I thought.

"Oh, I like being in people's dreams," I said, throwing the ball back to her.

"We were doing something in the kitchen," she said.

"What...?"

She laughed at my hesitation.

That morning, Mala asked Naomi to do some role-playing. Bryan McCarty played the role of me, as Naomi's husband. Mala had made a good choice for Naomi, for Bryan and I even looked a little like each other. We both had thin bodies, his perhaps more wiry muscular then mine, and we both had dark, full beards and similar straight noses and sensual mouths. We both had a quick smile and sense of humor and we both had protective walls around our feelings. Bryan loved the stars and planets in the sky and taught astronomy at a community college. He dodged his feelings by acting out in the external world. (Also, he sometimes acted with Portland's Storefront Theater.) When things got

127

weird, Bryan simply went out the window. I dodged my deeper feelings by looking them straight in the eye and denying them.

I watched carefully as Naomi acted out the anger and frustration she felt in our marriage. Bryan did good. He got angry back at her. She fed on that. It seemed so easy for Bryan. Why couldn't I do that? Naomi missed that in our marriage, I'm sure. She had grown up in a family where anger meant love. Anger meant attention. To me, anger meant my mother and father at the supper table, night after night, bickering at each other, year after year as I grew up in a little country town in Georgia. Anger meant my mother was weary with nerves frazzled, threatening to knock my head off if I didn't get out from under her feet. Anger meant she didn't want me around. A woman's anger meant the end of the world. So I had carefully avoided Naomi's anger and her long silences.

Her silences could last for days, even weeks.

I didn't know what to do or say. Gradually, I learned to walk around her walls. Just as I had learned to tiptoe around the house when my mother worked nights in the Douglasville cotton mill and needed to sleep during the day. With Naomi, I went on with my daily life, waiting for the ice to thaw, waiting for the warmness that I loved.

I felt afraid that Naomi might leave. She felt the same about me. Afraid that I would leave her for another woman. I didn't understand her fear, for I had no desire to be with another woman. Yet I couldn't convince her, I seemed ready at any moment to betray our marriage.

I couldn't be there for Naomi; not all of me.

I didn't understand why.

I felt the shame of not being enough for Naomi. In her role-playing with Bryan, she appeared so strong and beautiful, so much anger coming out. She looked like a princess. Others in the group noticed this too.

To choose a partner for our next exercise, I looked for Sandy. Another man had already nabbed her. I suddenly felt confused. I had no idea who to pick. The only thing Mala had told us was to choose a partner of the opposite sex. I didn't want to pair up with Naomi for this exercise, or any of the exercises. It felt too sticky. Already we had exchanged harsh words the night before, when I wanted to sleep with her.

Looking around, I saw the petite, dark-haired woman who had danced across the lawn during our lunch break. I had been sitting on the stairwell, feeling depressed and withdrawn. Glancing out a window, I had seen a beautiful woman skipping towards the meeting house. A sannyasin; she wore all burgundy-colored clothes. She had danced barefooted across the lawn, gathering her long burgundy skirt around her waist. She didn't have on any underwear, for all the world to see. I watched her until she reached the house and disappeared from sight. In that moment I envied her. "Envy no one"—"live by no man's code"—Bob Dylan had taught a whole generation this great lesson. Yet in that moment, I envied the woman's freedom. I envied the joy and careless abandonment she displayed as she danced across the grass.

"You want to?" I asked her.

"Sure," she said.

We stood there, waiting for instructions. Mala told everyone to hug their partners. The dark-haired woman and I hugged each other and then I didn't hear the rest of Mala's instructions. I felt this warm, feminine body embracing mine. I felt her heart beating close to mine, a woman who didn't even know me, and I couldn't stop from crying. I held onto her and cried and cried.

Help me, Mala.

Suddenly Mala was down on the floor, with someone else at my feet, someone at my head, and she worked on my chest with both hands.

"Breathe, David! Breathe!"

I lay on the floor a long time, crying. Mala kept working on my heart area with her hands, urging me to let the tears out, to let the pain and grief out.

Later, I walked down to the ocean. I saw the dark-haired woman on the beach. She shyly walked by me. We didn't speak. I learned that her name was Merika.

A few nights later, at home by the fire, Naomi opened a bottle of wine. Naomi didn't often drink, not even wine. I hadn't had a glass of wine in seven years, not since quitting both wine and weed while traveling in Greece. I poured myself a glass of wine.

We loved our talks. The talking seemed to bring us together. We just didn't know how to talk about our marriage. My feelings of being in an emotional cage. Her feelings of anger and disappointment. Things we couldn't escape. That's what going to Australia was all about. Escape from a world coming apart at the seams. Only we thought it was the other world. The world outside us. We didn't see the intersection coming up.

Naomi had researched everything. We got things ready. Everything except our souls. We even took a trip to San Francisco to see the Australian Consulate. Suddenly, the idea of immigrating to Australia sent her into a secret panic. Overnight, she changed her mind.

If seemed so crazy, not being able to talk about our marriage. We could love each other, night after night like pages in a storybook that you never want to end, and yet you're dying to know how to turns out. I thought the want between us would make everything okay and that we didn't need a backup. I thought that no matter what happens, the spirit fire between us would never go out. But the soul swings back and forth, as I was about to learn. For that is the nature of the soul. All that which explodes leads us to the Source. All that implodes, leads us to the Source. Above everything else, above even my love for Naomi, I felt the timeless calling of my soul, calling me homeward. Naomi must have heard the same calling and decided to give us a push.

Naomi liked the poem I had written for Sandy. What she did not like, what made her feel terribly sad, she said, was the fact that her husband could write this intimate and romantic poem to another woman. I had no quarrel with her feelings. I had my own pain and the dance, the wine, the fire, the poem—these gave me some place to step, if only for a moment, outside the pain.

I didn't plan to give Sandy the poem. I knew that could really create grief for me. And might even put Sandy off. After all, I was married and she might think I was being a little weird. Besides, Sandy had her own problems. She was stuck in a bad relationship, the kind I'd seen before. Her lover was having an affair with her best friend. You can bet your life savings I didn't want to touch that one.

"Can't we come ALIVE without going through all this pain?" Naomi wanted to know. "I'm tired of all this pain."

That night, and the nights to follow, Naomi and I had long talks by the fire about our marriage. Night after night I got raked over the coals. I couldn't argue with her accusations. After all, I had done such and such, when was it? Three years ago? Last week? Naomi's indictments overwhelmed me. She had such a way of making things so final. She kept hammering me and I kept taking it. I felt like I was swallowing swords.

§

**from *Going into the darkness* / *Tales of past times*
(an unpublished novel)**

Total Fire, Finally

(As told by his wife)

1

"STAMINA OF SURVIVORS TAXED BUT STILL FIRM"
blares the February 22 *Oregonian* headline

Yeah, he says, my eyes want to close, too

For Christmas, he gave me a new belt to keep
my pants up, and I gave him a set of
stacking dolls made in the USSR.
A doll within a doll within a doll within
a doll. "I'll be your," Dylan croons, "baby
tonight!" My lover gives me
a pair of used suspenders to keep
my pants up, I laugh, I don't seem to be
doing a good job of it.

2

RIGHT, WHAT'S LEFT

Existing on Murine, aspirin and strong cups of coffee
trying to kill myself on no sleep, cigarettes, wine
driving, driving, driving
no peace, all pieces, everything falls apart
this house, my car, my life, all pieces
everything I do is wrong, up and dressed by the time
he brings morning coffee, he wanted to sit in bed and talk
Thank you, I say, he turns his back and leaves the room
THANK YOU! I scream and he mumbles, you're welcome,

by this time tears down my face as I strip my clothes
off in emotional frustration, okay, we'll sit in bed and talk
all I wanted was a cup of coffee
(and I need ten more hours of sleep...)

My physical body is down to 103 pounds and struggles
to keep the pace, my emotional body is spent
my spiritual body hangs on by a thin thread
my intellectual body spins like a Whirling Dervish
finds no place to stop and rest
this bed feels like a truck stop now

Last night, he pours hot boiling water into my bath,
averting his eyes because he can't bear to see my nakedness
and furious because I'm writing, he thinks,
a letter to my lover halfway around the world,
gone to experience Tantric Meditation with
some unknown lady leaving
two here, experiencing celibacy within
marriage, marriage, marriage, what marriage?

My poet-husband reads a poem I wrote
I see the wheels turning in his head!
He's gonna steal my lines! That's what poets do
best, he laughs.

3

FINALLY, TOTAL FIRE

Very calmly, she folds the marriage certificate
in half...

tears it neatly on the fold, separating
the half signed by the Groom
from the half signed by the Bride.
Half of that is mine,
he said.

So she gave him his side
and with frustration, and in his quick anger
he crumples the paper and throws it
into the fireplace,
within seconds
transformed to smoke and ashes.

And she, with her deliberate
slowness
lights a corner by the small
flame of an orange candle
and after what seemed like Forever,
hers too, turned to ashes.

Very carefully, she placed the ashes
into an envelope and sealed it.
A reminder that once,
finally,
she'd seen the Total Fire.

Turning the wheel

Where are you running, Friend?
Where will you go to lose yourself
and find who you truly are?

To the Rajneesh Ashram in India?
One month in Poona and you grab the first flight out,
terrified for your life.

Will you go to Japan? Or to Europe,
or to Vermont in the fall;
or to Colorado,
to heal the roots you've been ground-burning
as quickly as they show?

Friend, you're running so fast
you've created a raging fire behind you,
and it is this fire you must go through,
to radiate light from the shadows of your heart.
(And you know this, don't you?)

What frightens you, Friend?
What makes you so desperate—like an outlaw?
and there is a natural law we cannot escape!—
that you run so fast you keep repeating yourself,
endlessly turning on the wheel.

Is it the thought of death? Of time running out?
Is it ego? Or desire? Or just jealousy?
Is it thirst or need or lust for power?
Or, like Oedipus, a roundabout journey
to the death of a man you never really knew?

Where are you running, Friend?
Where will you go to lose yourself
and find who you truly are?

All these things twice

You were stumbling a little,
to my surprise,
and singing:
"I want four walls around me,
to hold my life..."
Coming back from Caesar's Country Western Bar
& Dance,
do you remember walking in the park
and sitting beneath that giant fir tree,
and watching a city bus go by
as we talked about our marriage
and the night sky,
and wondering aloud
if, in ten years, we would remember
this, sitting in the park at night
a little drunk,
and a whole lot scared;
winter in the air
and the dry leaves thick on the grass
by the sidewalk,
do you remember?

*****

"I want to spend the night with Eden," Naomi told me.
She said it as if she were asking permission.
I stared at her. I didn't say anything.
"You don't need to worry," she said. "I'm not going to run off with him the way Angelina did."
Still, I said nothing as Naomi kept assuring me she wasn't like Angelina, that she wouldn't leave me. Going to Eden, getting to know him better before he left for India, this, she said, was something she needed to do.

What could I say? Yes, I could say, No.

But I wasn't her daddy.

How could I tell her what to do or not to do?

No more than I could tell Angelina, five years ago.

We had returned from Europe. "What do I do?" Angelina asked. I could only tell her what I would have told myself. And what I knew she would do anyway. "Follow your heart," I said. "That's what I've always done."

The affair between Eden and Angelina didn't last long. Which didn't surprise me. What surprised me was the attraction between them in the first place. They seemed to have little in common, other than their connection with me. Angelina and I belonged to the same spirit tribe. We were kindred souls. But not so much with Eden. Yet, I felt deeply drawn to the man, so why not Angelina? Maybe he challenged her on some level. Maybe she thought she could heal his wounded soul. For certainly she's a healer. And certainly Eden showed glimmers of light. But mostly, he lived in the shadows. (Don't worry, Merika. I tested him with a mirror, just to make sure.) I saw in him a great instinctual knowledge, and great power, and yet something had gone wrong. Something in him had gotten twisted, bent out of shape.

One weekend, several years before I married Angelina and went to Greece, a bunch of us were at the Oregon coast, climbing a long, grassy bluff that overlooked the ocean. We walked a path on a protected game reserve and a herd of wild goats scattered as we made our way up the thin footpath. Eden led the way, as if he had been chosen leader. He carried a wooden staff and, with his strong body, piercing eyes, and the coastal wind blowing his long, dark hair, he seemed like a reincarnation of Moses leading his people to the Promised Land. He had charisma and charm and he told great stories, lacing them with exaggerated humor or terror, or enthusiasm. "A beautiful asshole," that's how someone once described him.

In those days, I saw Eden Maldek as a seeker, a contemplative, a soul who had found himself—or lost himself—in this great mystery called life and, like myself, he was looking to make sense of it all. We didn't pal around together, and sometimes I wondered why not. I couldn't even get mad at him for what happened between him and Angelina. Those things happened. Especially back then. To all of us. We got bounced around like billiard balls all over the table. Or like small boats on a river in turbulent weather. And, no matter what happened, we knew that just around the next bend we'd find still another grand adventure. None of us had a permanent home. We had no allegiance to any cause except to experience life.

For all that Angelina meant to me, for all that I loved her, and for all the great and intense memories we shared together in Greece, life would go on. She was married when I first met her. You could say that what comes around goes around. We had found each other at the right time. We had traveled to Paris and backpacked over Europe. We had made love under the bluest skies in this world and swam naked in the sea that gave birth to Aphrodite. We had lost each other in Greece and had to face humpty dumpty dangers alone. Certainly, for myself, I had to go through trial by fire and water. We had been shattered and transformed, both of us. I mean, how much heaven and earth can a man and woman stand together?

Eventually, Eden and I got back together again as friends. He knew about Anna and me, about what had happened between us that summer I returned from Europe. He never really said anything, but I knew it pissed him off. Eden felt like a brother to me, yet, as the poet d. a. levy once said, during his slow suicide in Cleveland, Ohio—no doubt about the time his wife and another poet spent the night together smoking dope and screwing their brains out: "*If brothers were good for anything, God would have had one.*"

Maybe Eden carried a grudge against me for giving him an old TV set. This happened before I met Angelina. Eden had rented a small house in a nest of tall fir trees on the other side of Portland. I had a black and white TV I hardly ever watched. A big one, not a portable. Oh, I watched *Star Trek* returns some of the time, but mostly I shunned the damn thing. Like snakes, TVs fascinate us, don't they? I can't be in the same room with one on without my eyes going to it, no matter what's playing, so I just don't want the blasted thing in the house. TVs are like sugar. A little sugar on your breakfast cereal, how much harm can that do? However, to sit in front of a whole bowl of the white stuff and spoon it in like a good soup, that seems self-destructive to me.

Eden came home from work one day and found his house had burned to the ground. He lost practically everything he owned. They said the TV had caused the fire. Hey, just call us Tweedledum and Tweedledee.

However, there was a difference between us.

A real difference.

Eden carried a bitterness and a covert anger in his heart toward women. Most of the time, around me, he tried to keep this anger well hidden. He didn't want me to see this part of him, I later realized. He exposed his rage in casual slips here and there. Crude slips. Calling them "cunts." Mistrusting them. Using them. What shameful secret lay in his past? I wondered.

So, I stood there, bewildered and hurt, when Naomi told me she wanted to spend the night with Eden. I stood there silent, looking at Naomi, looking at history coming around again, looking at loss, looking at Naomi lying. Did she really think she could take a lover, just like that? Another woman might, yes. But I knew Naomi too well. I knew she couldn't love two men at once. No way.

Yet, she wanted me to believe this.

I suppose she wanted to believe this, too. Because Eden was leaving for India, perhaps that's why she thought she could sleep with him, that she could take a lover and still keep her marriage.

Finally I said: "Do what you need to do."

If I slept at all, I don't remember it. I got out of bed about five o'clock and made a cup of coffee. I built a fire. When Scotty woke, he found me sitting on the floor crying by the fire. He had never seen me cry before. He did the best thing he knew to do. He went and got his favorite big red truck and tried to get me to play. I hugged him for a moment.

"Where's Mom?"

139

"Oh, she's with a friend. She'll be home later."

He accepted that.

"I'll walk you to school this morning."

Scotty was a neat kid. But willful as hell. Always had been, since he could crawl, and he was always coming up with a slight-of-hand mind trick to get his way, as if he didn't think we could see his obvious manipulations. True to his Scorpio birthright, you could say, if you're inclined to speak in astrological concepts. And always testing his limits and believing that he had none. The time we went camping at Crater Lake, Scotty looked down from the guarded rim of the crater to the deep blue calm water of the lake and announced matter-of-factly: "I could climb down there." Yeah, right, Scotty.

This camping trip was the same trip the bear came into our campsite and ran off with our bag of bagels. The bear grabbed the bag of bagels as Naomi hurriedly put things into the back of our Datsun wagon, after we'd been warned by the Park Ranger about the bear. The bear dropped the bagels, but then came back—I suppose for the quart of milk. I grabbed my ax and chased him out of the camp and into the dark woods. Later that night, I hardly dared to fall asleep, thinking that only a canvas tent shielded us from the bear, should he attempt to break in. The night before, he had ripped into a tent across the road.

This last Christmas Day, Scotty went outside the house to play. He was on the sidewalk and I stood on our front porch watching him. A girl his own age came up to him. I'd never seen the girl before.

Little girl: "What's your name?"

Scotty: "If I tell you my name, will you be my friend?"

Little girl: "Sure."

Scotty (with emphasis): "My name is Godzilla!"

The little girl quickly left.

I remember how surprised I was to hear his first spoken sentence. He was looking out the window at a bird in a tree. Suddenly he cried, "Bird go bye-bye!" Another time, right after Mt. St. Helens blew her top and covered our North Portland house and most of the city in ash, we were standing across the street with some neighbors watching a new giant plume of smoke shoot into the air above the volcano. Scotty got concerned. "Why do we let the volcano do that?" he asked.

"Well, Scotty..."

*****

I walked Scotty and his friend, Cary, to school. I had already called in sick for work. When I got back from school, Naomi was home. Her hair was still damp from a shower.

"I took Scotty to school." That's all I said.

I wanted a cup of tea.

In spite of my pain and humiliation, I felt glad to see her. The panic inside me went away. I knew, however, that she needed anger, not hurt, not tears, not vulnerability.

By the time I made tea, my sadness turned to anger. "Goddamnit!" I swore at her.

Naomi kept looking at me, her gaze unwavering.

I didn't ask her what had happened.

"Even now I desire you," I told her.

"Well, I should hope so," she replied.

I flew out of my chair and grabbed her. We kissed crazily as I pushed my hand into her jeans. She came alive, wet, hot. I pulled her into our bedroom, knocking over a chair as I went. I flung her onto the bed. I ripped her flannel shirt off in one yank, buttons flying across the bed. I pulled her jeans and panties down and tossed them on the floor. I rolled her over, face down on the bed.

I took my belt from my jeans. I had never hit a woman in my life. I had no desire to hurt Naomi. Yet, what I did next seemed right to me. Even in my show of anger, however, I felt like an actor. I felt confused, not understanding what she really wanted from me. Recently, since this thing between her and Eden, our love making had changed. We played a game that she initiated. She called this game, "Taking it, if I want it." She would struggle with me and push me away and wouldn't open her legs. I had to overcome her, which wasn't always that easy,

141

before she would take me inside her. I smacked her several times across her buttocks. Hard enough that her lover would see marks the next time he fucked her. Naomi rolled over. She looked at me. She didn't utter a word. I grabbed her and kissed her mouth. Her beautiful, sweet mouth. She opened her legs for me. I licked her pussy and she was dripping wet. I sucked her and she started coming.

"Fuck me, fuck me," she whispered.

*****

"The only way I can stay in this house is to not feel guilty," she said.

Naomi wanted me to trust her.

I trusted her, but why the phone call from Eden in San Francisco that I only learned about by accident, by a "slip of the tongue"?

Eden had gone to San Francisco to clear legal stuff for his trip to India. Molly had finally sent him his passport. Before, Naomi would have been excited to hear from Eden and would have immediately told me that he had called her from San Francisco. Ah, but now that he was her lover....

And then came the Special Delivery letter with the key to Eden's van, a letter he thought I wouldn't see, and which Naomi obviously wasn't about to mention.

And the next nine days?

She drove to Eugene for her Thursday night class and told me she'd see me sometime on the weekend. I knew she had plans to take photographs of Mala and Aniruddha, and of Mala's little boy, who was dying. Mala had returned from India because of her little boy's health. "Go back to America. You belong with your son," Bhagwan had told her. I knew also that Eden was suppose to leave San Francisco on Thursday by train, to come back to Portland.

She did mention that she'd probably see Eden before me.

I didn't doubt that.

Then I got a call from Julie, a sannyasin friend in Naomi's psychic development class. She wanted to talk to Naomi. Julie had already talked to Mala. No one knew where Naomi had gone. She stayed gone for

142

nine days. The night they returned, Eden took off for India. And I learned that later on, Naomi would be going, too.

A small fire flickered in the fireplace beside us. The same fireplace where we had spent so many winter evenings together, drinking coffee, chatting, watching TV, making love. Naomi had made her sleeping bag into a bed near the fireplace after she had moved out of our bedroom, after she and Eden had become lovers. One night, after Eden had been in India for several weeks, she was lying on her sleeping bag in her nightgown, smoking a cigarette and watching *Doctor Zhivago* on TV. I crawled across the floor, the brown, carpeted floor of our home, begging for her pussy, begging for a taste of her sweet, dark love, moist and cruel as spring earth in April rain. I crawled on my hands and knees, just to see how far I would go, just to see how far she would go. Please, please... my heart ripping apart, splitting me into a creature as ancient as the ocean floors. She raised her gown and opened her legs for me. I put my lips to her yoni. "David," she said, turning the other way, scorn and indifference blasting like thunderbolts in her earth-burning eyes, "I'd rather fuck someone off the street than you."

What kept me on the line?

My fear of losing her. Naomi knew that and she worked it well. She was always going to leave. I suspected that she wanted to leave me before I could leave her. We human beings do get complicated, don't we? Not so much in essentials, but in our shapes and forms. In a power struggle, we'll do whatever gives us the illusion of having the upper hand, even if that means killing everything that ever meant anything to us.

Looking back, I think we both did our best, intentionally or unintentionally, to tear everything apart, everything good between us and everything bad. Everything.

§

from *Going into the darkness* / *Tales of past times*
(an unpublished novel)

143

The last thing on his mind

They closed two places that night;
a bottle of dry red wine from Greece
at Poppi's,
then white retsina,
which, to his amazement,
she relished with the first glass—
a woman after his heart! he thought.
She talked about her husband,
a "business partner" she called him,
and, like any woman, she wanted to be wanted;
and he talked about his wife
and her love affair with his friend,
their coming divorce, her name change
to Sister and travel plans for India
to be with her lover, already there.

But it was all craziness, he thought
and they still loved each other.
Two nights ago,
the first night since her lover
flew off to India,
they made love and he swore
he could never go to bed with another
woman, he loved her that much.
And these words opened a door back
to their marriage, after India.
If she went to India. Now
she wavered. Or so she said.
But he only found that out later,
the night she burned their marriage
certificate, and then carefully, very carefully,
—oh, she knew how to twist the knife—
put the ashes into an envelope,
perhaps to scatter over the Ganges,
but he never asked.

144

It felt ALL crazy,
and they were too, time
the waiter put the chairs upside down
on the tables and it was the last thing on his mind,
to make love to her that night.
But they kissed under a street light
on the way to Aunt Lucie Divine,
and both knew there was no turning back,
though they spoke not a word
of what might be.

"I could never have an affair,"
she had said to him in Poppi's
(but with no reference to him;
they felt safe with each other)
"without first telling my husband."

But the word never, like forever,
rang and rang and rang in his mind.
Where had he heard that before?
Why, only a few weeks ago, his wife
had vowed she could never…
And just two nights ago, he swore
he could never….

They closed Aunt Lucie Divine
and where to go?
He was staying with friends
—they were in Eugene
for a weekend spiritual retreat,
and his "assignment" for the night
was to drink a bottle of wine with her
(one bottle)
and she, to use her intuition.
She had a bottle of Sauvignon Blanc

back at her motel,
so they walked in the February night
holding hands, laughing,
not thinking too much, not analyzing,
not feeling the pain
and confusion of his wife leaving,
or the boredom and frustration
of loving a husband never there.

Inside,
beneath the "proper English lady,"
in her pride and her well-cared garden,
beneath the white high-button collar,
beneath years of making appearances
and holding her intensity
with acceptable pretenses
and half-hearted attempts at being,
a wild woman was coming alive,
and wanted out, wanted to be free;
ached to be desired;
and not assumed, not taken for anything,
or compromised, or denied, or put aside;
but allowed TO BE.

*****

He woke her in the nicest way,
touching her body like flickering warm sunlight
through a curtain of dream,
and she loved every moment of this moment
and laughed and let him have his way,
all the burning in his kisses awakening
her to life.

"It's time you come to your own,"
she whispered, her voice

cutting through all his remembrances,
his shame and childhood prisons,
and blessing him with forgiveness,
such that he would always come back
to this voice,
in the days and nights that would follow.

"Do you feel guilty?" he asked.
"No, I feel marvelous!" And she laughed.
He grinned back at her.
"You're too damn healthy!" he said.
"Of course I'll have to look him in the face
when I go home, and tell him. And you?"
"No, no. I feel great.
But for this slight headache."
All that wine and seven years of not drinking;
two hours of sleep,
and the delight of her energy with his.
Considering this,
what had he to complain of?

They were the first guests to arrive
at the retreat house,
a big Victorian house on 14th street,
and they warmed themselves by the fire.
(Aniruddha loved to build devilish fires.
They had things in common, these two men.)

And then his wife drove up.

I'm leaving

Naomi didn't participate in this weekend group. She did, however, volunteer to prepare lunch both days for the group. Naomi had made plans to go to Bhagwan's ashram in Poona. She and Julie were going together. They needed to go *right now*, Naomi explained to me. One, they could get a price break on the plane ticket; and two, they wanted to arrive before the intolerable hot weather set in; and, three, she had a friend to travel with, blah blah blah. Eden, being in Poona, had little to do with her decision to go to India, you understand. That is, until he calls her from Poona to tell her that he can't stand the place and that he's coming back to Portland. Naomi immediately cancelled her plans to go to India.

Marcia was the last straw for Naomi. Naomi still wanted to believe we might get back together after she came back from India.

"What you did with Marcia," she told me," closed that door."

Perhaps Mala thought I had acted with courage, doing what I did to free us from the sticky ball of string that Naomi and I had created in our marriage. We were nesting in our own emotional shit. As for myself, I didn't see any act of courage. What else could I do?

In three days, Naomi and I got a divorce.

Naomi wrote the papers herself.

I agreed to lie to the judge. Naomi and I told the judge that she was pregnant by her lover—and for sure the baby was his—and that she wanted to go to India to be with him.

Could this divorce be saved?

Aniruddha wanted to hold some psychic classes in Portland. I offered him our house, since Naomi would soon be going off to India. The day Aniruddha arrived in Portland, Naomi came to our house to see him. Aniruddha had an intense talk with the two of us. He gave us his best shot. He had Naomi role-playing both herself and me—or her image of me. Back and forth she kept going in her roles. Back and forth. Aniruddha (God bless him) told her she was running away from her problem, but she seemed determined not to change her mind. I knew she wouldn't give up Eden. I knew this but didn't say it.

The next morning, Naomi called me.

During the night she had written me a long letter. In her letter, she wrote how she loved me, how she needed me, and that she wanted to work on our relationship. She felt scared, too. Maybe for the first time, I thought. For she knew she would have to finally confront her own patterns of avoidance. Yet, I wonder if she felt fear for another reason. Perhaps deep within she knew staying with me was not the right choice for her, and to stay with me meant denying her true, evolving self. The untraveled road of her destiny had taken a different turn, and go she must, no matter what, no matter who, no matter the cost. Indeed, I loved her for that very strength and passion.

She brought the letter to me.

I could hardly believe it. So much we needed to do, so much we needed to say to each other, so many sticky strings to untangle, carefully, lovingly.

She brought a few personal things with her.

That night, Eden called from Salt Lake City.

He would arrive in Portland at midnight.

"You're fucking me over, Naomi," Eden muttered.

The three of us were sitting in a bar. We had stopped to talk after picking up Eden at the airport. He was pissed off. He wanted a whiskey and he seemed weirded out by India. I guess he couldn't leave India fast enough. Well, Eden, what did you expect?

I looked at him closely.

We were inside each other. We were parts of each other. Yet we were opposites. Like Cain and Abel. I was a giver, a pleaser, the Good Boy. The voice of reason. The one who understands. The one who accepts. The one who'd rather hurt himself than harm another. Eden was a taker, a manipulator, the Bad Boy. The Dark One. A man of mystery and danger. Ice and shadows. Hardness like a mirror. Never open. Never showing what he is. An act of revenge. A man dense with his rage of childhood abuse. The infant destroyer. A psychopath willing to attack and hurt with his power. An arrogant motherfucker. A

149

hidden fist. A beautiful promise that would never be kept. He was like a thief at a wedding banquet stuffing things under his coat. He would leave with his coat stuffed and a victorious grin, but he would leave with an empty stomach. He was a hunter and he lived for the kill. Like a drug, the hunt gave him hope. The hunt gave him a rush. He came alive inside. He lit up with power. Once he caught the prey, however, for him the game was over. The game was finished. (A hard lesson that Naomi would have to learn.)

I knew our friendship had come to an end.

He had written me from India that he would choose Naomi over me if it came to that. As a man I understood this. And of course it came to this.

Naomi stayed the night with me.

Aniruddha had scheduled some personal readings for the next morning. Marcia came to see him for a reading. Naomi freaked out when she saw Marcia. Before I knew it, Naomi left the house through a side window. I ran after her car, yelling for her to stop. I chased her until my lungs gave out.

The next day she came by the house while I was at work.

She left a brief note. "No more yo-yo," she wrote. "I'm leaving."

§

**from *Going into the darkness / Tales of past times*
(an unpublished novel)**

Going

Where to go,
now that you're not
going with me?

Where to go,
now that you've made
up your mind
to leave;
you,
who, more than any other
being alive
have touched me
with the touch of fire:
a deep blue flame rising
from below,
into my heart,
an intense rose, radiant,
burning into a luminous red orange
light, an electrical egg around
my body, a flame,
singing,
        singing.

Where to go,
now that you're gone?
I shall not repeat
myself,
forever.

The game of love,
exhausted;
the child we never

had,
the garden
and fruit trees:
paths
I will not travel
with you this time,
all turning to ash
in my hands,
like in the dream
I once had in Greece—
the meaning of my life
in a handful of ashes.

And you?

Where will you
go?
What will you do?

To India,
to be with your lover?
Already you see auras,
read past lives,
and feel the exquisite heart
beat of each moment,
with your own winged heart.
Perhaps,
(if you go),
you'll return a healer
of souls,
a transformer of lives.

Perhaps,
(a personal sentiment
now),
with someone else, another
man,
you will have your flowers,
your fruit trees and green beans
to put up in the summer,
your tasseled corn,
your sweet red strawberries.

But the fire!
The fire will forever
be
you and me,
a living, flowering flame,
you and me,
our loving, merging,
a crying,
a dancing birth &
death between
us,
through us
and within us, around
us,
singing,
     singing,
singing,
     singing

Going into the darkness

1981-1985

§

To equate light with love is misdirected.
For certainly there's as much love in darkness
as there is in light.
—Alora, in conversation

Every major galaxy, it turns out,
has a black hole at its core.
—Robert Irion, "Homing in on Black Holes,"
The Smithsonian, April 2008

The scholars are deficient in that they are afraid to enter
the darkness.
Reason shuns it and is afraid to steal in.
But in avoiding the darkness reason does not arrive
at a vision of the invisible.
—Nicholas of Cusa, 15th c.
Meditations with Nicholas of Cusa
trans. James Francis Yockey

As night descends

What to do?
Get drunk? Meditate? Go south?

It's June.
Been raining for days.
A fire blazing. Myself at a loss.

Maybe the radio?

"Just a little bit...!"
A blues/black chick shouting.

Damn, maybe that's what I need.
Three months celibacy.
(It gets easier, I'm told.
Celibacy that is.)
What the hell, this ain't jail.

Silence.

Only the fire crackling
& my thoughts

at a biological loss.

As night descends.

Drawing people out

"There's no
pretending in this world.
It's all an antidote,
Not a cure."

***

Wordy,
I'm too wordy,
Becky tells me &
lights a cigarette
& says, "I'm in a
very strange state."
.....
"Yes, I'm so literal
here."
And puffs
her white cigarette
& draws a picture
of Here & Now
in vivid colors.
A childhood dream?
A child dreaming.

"Death I accept
as I accept life."

***

"I feel really gypsy,"
she says.
"Gentle, gentle!" I tell her,
watching her hard press the crayons.
"No, it isn't gentle at all," she says.

"It's very harsh.
Isn't that ugly? It's
pretty!"

?

"Are you done?"

She looks up.
"Oh, no.
Going over the lines,
that's a way of life with
me!" She laughs,
grapping a purple crayon.

Becky was going blind. Is
that what she meant?

"I like that music!"
(It was Doug Kershaw
playing "Swamp Dance"
from *Days of Heaven*.)

Becky laughs loudly. "Oh, well,
we knew what we meant."

*****

"It's a riot,
that's what it is," she says,
after going through all
the purples & blues,
then dumping the crayons out,

"I think we're almost at the end
of the rainbow."

Becky holds her picture up.
"It's a floating kite," I say,
thinking of the ancient Chinese
and their Floating World.
"A Viking ship, too," she says.

*****

"The game is drawing people out."

You knew

Your dark, smoky eyes,
the way you looked into me,
you knew I had drifted and stumbled
through this passing world,
a little dazed,
looking for What?

Just to catch a glimpse of you,
in your purple shirt & tight faded jeans,
& your sensual body, earthy, evanescent,
a gypsy, a sorceress (I fantasized),
& on your right hand
you wore two plain silver rings
& on your left, your wedding finger,
an elaborate, occult ring with three stones
set across a silver band,
& a silver bracelet
with a single turquoise teardrop.

You paid with crisp new dollars, I watched you,
almost $30 of bread, meat, things that go in a home,
too much for one person alone;
& I with only a bottle of cheap red wine,
a bunch of bananas,
a box of stoned wheat crackers—
not even some cheese
to give the illusion of a future possibility.

But you knew.

Your dark, smoky eyes,
you looked straight into mine & Jesus,

I had to turn away, the intensity
of time & beginnings & incandescent promises;
& for what?
We shall never see each other again,
but just the same you looked into me,
& you smiled,
& you knew, oh, you knew.

Thinking of Helen on an island off Greece

A bronze statue of a slender girl with braids
running all the way down her back,
thin legs,
and full, heavy breasts,
a pensive look on her face—
this bronze girl that captured my eyes
in the Portland Art Museum—
reminds me of a woman in love with Greece
and of a time gone by;
her dreams of a lasting marriage disappearing
out the door
without even a word of farewell, or how come,
or I'll send for my clothes.

But now she can stash her money, you see, and go to
Greece.
(What little there remains after rent and food and
gasoline.)
How fortunate her dissolution!

Only I think she does not see it this way.

And who can blame Helen her anger,
her hostility?
She looks gentle, this girl raised on a ranch in Montana;
this woman who listens to old Hank Williams songs
and whose house is overrun with stray cats;
a lover of streams and gardens and climbing hills,
an intellectual creature who would be tough,
hard as spikes on glowing embers beneath running feet;
but bitter, this look in her eyes now, this betrayed woman,

always holding herself in, stoical,
her sweet mouth tightening into determined lines of grief.

So we will pass each other, this time around, this woman
and I, in this dark, crazy night of the soul, each to each,
and I will ponder (this one time only),
what might have been,
in a blazing noonday sun on an island off Greece.

*****

Did Helen ever get to Greece?

I don't know. We didn't see each for very long. When I asked her over the phone why she didn't want to see my anymore, she answered, "I got scared."

I know I came into her life at a difficult time. But she liked how I could see into her heart. She liked being respected and appreciated by a man, something she wasn't used to, being respected and appreciated by a man. She let her guard down for a moment.

I don't think she had ever met anyone who could see through her walls. While we talked quietly together that first time, I looked into her, I don't know how, I just did it. I don't even remember the words that came out of my mouth. I do remember telling her about her fears, about what she wanted, about how she protected her gentleness, about how she hid her true feelings.

"Who are you?" she asked, half-jokingly.

"I'm a fictitious character," I answered, half-seriously.

"In whose book?" she asked, arching her eyebrows.

"In this book," I grinned at her.

Most of the time, you know, we talk to each other and to ourselves through this protective screen, this wall of core beliefs (conscious and unconscious). For something new to get through this screen probably takes as much energy and persistence and timing as a Chinook salmon

164

swimming up the Columbia River and fighting the great Bonneville Dam and The Dalles, just to get to its spawning grounds. This perceptual screen, this personal language, as does our communal language, determines, I believe, mostly what we see and don't see. Is this good or bad? Certainly we need gate keepers or we would probably go mad, so much energy data flowing into us. As T. S. Eliot said, "Mankind can stand only so much truth." Yet, to really listen to another being, to really hear another person, we must allow gaps into our screen, little passages of free-flowing energy, respectful places of silence. In other words: emptiness. To do this, we must cultivate an awareness of our own personal bias as well as our cultural and social and biological bias: a sense of our own distortions. After all, who can say, except in a limited sense, what's true and what's false, as if life were a test? Seeing into Helen's mind and her unacted desires and then getting into a brief relationship with her, getting past her protective veils, I found out, were two different things altogether.

Even with Naomi I never considered our differences, not really. Certainly not as an issue. I thought that love between a man and a woman could overcome whatever differences. If they wanted each other enough. It's kind of like the religious trap: If only we had more faith. If only we had more love. If only we had more knowledge. If only we had more of this or more of that, nothing bad would ever happen to us. We could control our fates. We could control the universe.

Even in my romantic relationship with Alora, I sidestepped our differences. We had so much in common. Or so we did at the time. We certainly cared for each other. We had a commitment to the body between us. We both loved books. We loved traveling. We loved plants and gardening. We loved Spirit. But, most of all, as a couple, we shared an intense, common focus: emotional healing.

Alora's the one who introduced me to the spiritual warrior teacher that would save my life. You might say I turned into one of her star pupils. Harriet Douthitt welcomed me with fire and water and earth and sprit and I had no other place to go. I had run out of places to hide.

165

Harriet inspired me to acknowledge my fear: to acknowledge my anger: to acknowledge my love: to acknowledge ALL my feelings. She taught me to feel. For Harriet inspired me to remember. To remember *who I am.*

Harriet terrified me. She saw right through my defenses and my denials. This woman, who once told me, "I took my first darshan on a barstool in Memphis," could open up the abyss inside me right before my eyes and I could not shut down my heart to the pain and sadness imprisoned inside my body, nor to the terrifying spiritual love I felt in her presence. This beautiful, willowy, blue-jeaned blonde with a Southern accent and a swaying rhythm in her hips when she walked, zoomed right past the inner child and went straight to the terrified baby inside me. The baby wanting unconditional love from Mom. And from all women. Every moment. All the time. And not finding this love available. For every reason in the world. And none of these reasons meant anything to a baby. The man-child who learned to shut down joy and avoid anger and tiptoe around his mother and father. The man-child who learned to hide his spirit force, to protect his spirit force from prying eyes, who built a hard shell around his heart and who, because he could not go the way of the predator, the conqueror, the seducer, due to his own nature and awareness, for he truly wanted connection, he truly wanted to feel love, but, and he never forgot this, he never lost this divine remembrance: love meant openness, and openness meant vulnerability and, in this world, in this heavy density of bodies and egos and power struggles, vulnerability meant attack; and so he turned his life into a search and a way out and every event into a conflict and a struggle between spirit and body and every chance encounter and gesture and look into an invitation and a dance, and a sexual flowering into the soul of a woman, for he truly loved women, he truly wanted to share power, and he wanted to live in balance, and he wanted to come home.

Once, at a party with Alora, early in our relationship, I suddenly felt this great need to go home. The party had been given in Alora's honor. When we first met, she worked with troubled teens. Some weekends she

166

stayed as a supervisor of a half-way house. When she quit this job, her co-workers threw her a going-away party. I went to the party, not because I really wanted to go to the party, but because she asked me to.

At first, I enjoyed the party. Then I found myself withdrawing, getting bored. I picked up a book and sat reading alone on the sofa. Suddenly, I felt myself in emotional pain, almost in tears. Alora noticed my discomfort.

"What's going on?" she asked, concern in her voice.

"I want to go home," I said.

As we walked out the door to go home, I felt comforted.

I remembered this incident two years later when, lying on the bed in our home, my mind and heart deeply opened to the world of love within me, once again I cried out, "I want to go home."

I wanted to go home.

But I was home. I realized then that my desire for home, now and the time before, had little to do with the house I lived in. Alora and I had made a home together. As she held me in her arms, as I cried out I wanted to go home, I knew home meant more than this body, this bed, this house, this country, this earth. Home means *who I am*.

Harriet would tell us: "If you're not vibrating unconditional love, you're in stuff." Most of the time we're in stuff. Hell, maybe all the time. Raw, sewage stuff. The stuff underneath the false smile, the hidden hand, the guilty mind. The stuff called the Other. The stuff called wars. The stuff called social consciousness. The stuff called sexism. The stuff called racism. The stuff the world is made of. The stuff called power over. The stuff called ego. The stuff we bargain with for love. The stuff we sell for love. The stuff we hide, the stuff we keep. The stuff called the search for truth. The stuff called doing good, doing bad. We might feed the poor, we might sell life insurance, we might write books and talk to God. We might save the whales; we might honor the land; we might travel to the moon; we might be right or we might be wrong: no matter, if we're not vibrating pure love, if we're not vibrating Spirit, we're in stuff, we're not real, we live in shadows, we live in fear.

Only later, with Liana, did I learn this painful truth about romantic relationships: sometimes, no matter how much you care for each other, you can't sleep in the same bed.

In the beginning, Liana could list ninety-nine reasons she loved me. And she did. I felt so appreciated, so recognized. Liana was definitely a great listener. Yet, I kept waiting for the other shoe to drop. And in the end, Liana, leaving no stone unturned, could cite just as many reasons to cheerfully strangle me.

What's the point? I asked myself. We had tried everything. At least that's how I felt. We read books from mainstream to New Age. We read every book I'm ever going to read on relationships. We did their exercises. We discussed their theories. We took long walks. We mirrored, we negotiated, we listened, we joked, we talked, we quarreled, we prayed. We even went to see a counselor with a PhD in psychology. I did inner child work and personal channeling and meditated every day. Liana did inner child work and women's stuff and took care of her dog.

For three years we struggled. We couldn't even agree to live together. We mostly saw each other only on weekends; or every other weekend. Liana needed lots of rest. I had no problem with that. Liana worked as a physician and she had rheumatoid arthritis. She had been divorced not more than a year—yes, I should have known better—that's not enough time to get over the hurt and disillusionment of a true love gone south—and, most of the time during her marriage, her rheumatoid arthritis had gone undiagnosed. This secret drain on her energy caused great conflict in her marriage. Now, she saw herself as "damaged goods." In the beginning of our relationship, she was an emotional basket case. She cried at the drop of a hat and she carried so much anger and frustration over the divorce and the way her marriage had ended. She was pumping it up, acting out her emotions, rather than deeply feeling her feelings inside her. That's how I saw it. But after all my work with Harriet, and dealing with the fear that a woman's anger had always inspired in me, I had no fear or hesitation about working with Liana's anger and her tears. When we finally broke up, she had regained her self-confidence. Once more, and even more than before, Liana's presence resonated a strong and beautiful and powerful woman.

We had sweet and wonderful sex when we had sex. But when the pain outweighs the joy, with no break in sight, and when the bright star called Eros has collapsed into a black hole, with no source or center or nurture, no intimacy, no renewal, no communication—*Did I say that? Did you say that? What did you say? I didn't say that, that's not what I meant, that's not what I meant at all*—what's the point?

So, we called it quits. Our differences had undone us. And our continuous struggle had undone something else within me, something so basic to my beliefs about romantic relationships that I no longer had the least desire to persuade or talk any woman out of her doubts or misgivings or hesitations or second thoughts. If you can't enter wholeheartedly, don't enter.

Do what you will. It happens or it doesn't. That's all.

§

**from *Going into the darkness / Tales of past times*
(an unpublished novel)**

A bone for the dogs

Today,
I just want to sit,
like the poet Neruda would sit,
deep in his thoughts of Chile
and the ocean and shoes.
I want to feel the breath of solitude,
like Castaneda in the desert at night,
listening to the heartbeat
of a moth.
I want to remember the Aegean Sea,
this ancient sea,
before it was invaded
by a surf of oil
and makeshift huts upon the shore;
and I want to walk
along the Great Coral Reef
and ponder a new world,
in reality.
I want to drink strong, black coffee,
the way Gurdjieff did,
(so they say),
and sit with Henry Miller
in Paris, in a cafe
before the War,
before he went to Greece.
I want to sit like Chief Joseph,
who traveled freely among his people
—when this land was free.
I want to sit like Bodhidharma,
alone for 20 years,
without eating or shitting or masturbating.
(No one even knew Bodhidharma was there

170

under the tree. They saw only the tree
and the shadow of the tree.)
I want to sit quiet as a tear
on the cheek of Christ.
I want to drink this bitter cup;
I want to feel my aloneness,
without thoughts of bare bosoms
and the burning bushes of youth
and tomorrow; pleasure
and pain, we are constant worlds
entwined with nature's vines,
roots; flowers that fly away
in remote jungles; dinosaurs
that rule the world with profit
and greed and patriotism on their lips.
I want to sit, to know my aloneness,
to ask questions one must answer alone
to oneself, awakening
from the years of false pretenses;
the sham beliefs I have been taught,
the limitations I have chosen.

    ***

Desires come and go,
I do not detain them.
But I will sit here, quietly
listening to this passing world:
the noise of a car going by;
a dog barking angrily; a boy
playing on the sidewalk;
the rain dripping off the gutters;
the slow Oregon rain that falls

like a soft funeral train,
like the tenderness of a sweet friend
who died long ago.
I will sit here,
calm in this moment of solitude;
my individuality a bone for the dogs
that would devour us,
for those who would feast upon the earth
and perish of famine in their souls,
for those who would tear out my
heart (if they could),
in the name of brotherhood,
Mother, Father, God.
I will sit here, lofty
in my heart as the redwoods,
unobtrusive as a shrub or
an ancient, gnarled olive tree,
invisible as truth,
mysterious as life, unknown,
lyrical.

Going into the darkness

"To equate light with love is misdirected," Alora once told me. "For certainly there's as much love in darkness as there is in light." Going into the darkness, I didn't know what to expect. I had some vague, romantic notion, I suppose, that going into the shadowlands of my own being could be done with a light held fast in my hands. Or strapped to my head like a miner's lamp. I didn't really want to go into the darkness without a light. Without a guide. That felt too scary.

But how else y'gonna go, Rimbaud?

I imagined I had even found a spirit guide to hold my hand on this journey. Like Dante's Beatrice. *The old man and the young girl...* I remembered writing this poem when I was twenty-two years old. *The old man and the young girl...* the old man who represented wisdom and knowledge through experience; the young girl who represented promise and hope and immortality. Was China this young girl that my intuitive vision had seen so long ago? A woman who could travel out-of-body. A woman who had not understood her ability to travel this way and who had given up this childhood gift when she entered college and majored in psychology.

Between worlds

"David. Wake up."

I opened my eyes slowly, not wanting to let go of the dream.

But more than anything, I wanted to see her again.

"It's you," I whispered, a little stunned.

"Of course it's me."

"I mean, the girl in my dream."

"Well, I hope you had a sexy dream." She smiled mischievously. "I've got to go now," she said. "It's almost seven. My little girl will be waking soon."

"She's at your grandmother's, right?"

As I let go of the dream, I remembered the night before.

China... I'll call her .

That's not her given name but it suits her.

We met in a smoky piano bar. My friend, Melina Foster, and I had been to an art theater to see a black and white Spanish film called *The Sargossa Manuscript*, one of the most amazing films—along with *El Topo*—I had ever seen. On the way home, we stopped in at a restaurant bar near where we lived, sharing a house, along with another friend, Jan Nelson. Melina ordered a gin and tonic, her favorite drink, and I ordered a glass of house red. We sat quietly talking at a table near the bar and I noticed a woman at the bar the same time she noticed me. Actually, I looked her way because I overheard her talking and her voice brought back a flood of memories. Her voice reminded me of Christine Isbell, a woman I had known for two weeks (and loved) years before, while traveling in Greece. I had never picked up a woman in a bar. I had never even gone into a bar with that thought in mind. I don't really care for bars. Sure, in my university days in Eugene, I drifted into Max's almost every night. But that was different. I had never picked up a woman in a bar, but I knew I couldn't just walk out and not talk to this woman. I got up and went to the men's room, because to go to the restroom I had to walk by the bar. The woman and I glanced curiously at each other. Coming back from the men's room, our eyes touched again and I murmured to her, "I'll come back."

"Ready to go?" I asked Melina.

"Sure."

Melina didn't care much for bars either. Why we stopped, just a fluke, I guess.

Melina had noticed the connection between me and the woman at the bar. She didn't say anything though. I think Melina had given up long ago on understanding the romantic entanglements that I got myself into.

I dropped Melina off at our house, not far from the restaurant, and then drove back to the bar.

Would she still be there?

Would she remember me? Would she have a man?

I didn't know the rules of meeting a woman in a bar, if such etiquette did exist.

The woman didn't seem surprised when I showed up. She didn't seem indifferent, but she didn't seem that excited. I didn't know how to read her, or the situation. I only knew my feelings, and my feelings urged me in the direction of this woman.

I sat down beside her. I ordered a glass of wine.

We looked at each other.

"Can I buy you a drink?" I asked.

She told me what she wanted.

Some strange name I'd never heard of.

A young black man dressed in a tuxedo came out and sat at the piano and started to play. We got our drinks and moved over to the piano. And that's where we stayed until the place closed, chatting and joking with the piano man. A good-looking dude, too. He seemed to know her. What if they had an understanding? Am I being stupid? Do I go? Do I stay? Back and forth I went. What's she's doing here anyway? She's not really looking for company. But I can't just let her go; I might never see her again.

So I kept hanging in there, waiting for some signal.

We danced together near the piano.

The piano man seemed to be on my side. He wanted to get us together. Softly he sang a French song, "Ne Me Quitte Pas," a song that Nina Simone had made famous on her album *I Put A Spell On You*. Maybe he was just a romantic, the piano man. Maybe we were all romantics, caught in a smoky web of time, just a boy and a girl in an old-fashioned movie with the piano man playing Sam Cupid, playing romantic songs like "Stardust" and "How Deep Is The Ocean," drawing us together in the shadows.

Come two o'clock the bar closed.

What do I do now? I still didn't know.

She seemed as uncertain as me. "You have a way home?" I asked.

She nodded. "My car's out front."

"What do you want to do?" I asked.

She didn't answer at first. Then, more to herself than to me, she said, "Why not? Why not do something daring?"

I waited.

"I drove my mother's car. Follow me and I'll drop it off."

I walked China to her car and then followed her for about a mile to her mother's place. Damn, the speed she drove and all the turns she made, I thought I might lose her. Did she want to lose me? I wondered. Hell, maybe she shouldn't even be driving.

China had a five year-old daughter. Her daughter was staying at her grandmother's for the weekend she told me. China lived in the same apartment complex as her mother.

China parked her mother's car and then we drove to my house. We tiptoed quietly up the stairs. China paused to admire a large oak-framed print I had hanging on my bedroom wall. It was a painting by Adolphe-William Baugureau of a beautiful, half-naked young woman fending off Cupid. The woman in the painting has both arms outstretched against Cupid's shoulder and Cupid, a naked, white-winged, boyish-looking cherub, has an arrow in one hand, poised above the woman's heart. The young woman has a smile on her lips, as if she's playing a delightful game with her small brother. I like Baugureau. I had picked up this print at the J. Paul Getty Museum in Malibu when Melina and I drove down to Ojai in the spring to attend a series of J. Krishnamurti talks.

I was living on the second floor of our house. I had a bedroom, a bath, and a small room I used as a writing room. Melina lived downstairs in the main bedroom and had a bedroom she used as a studio. Jan Nelson lived in the basement. Jan had just finished her medical internship. She was a surgeon. Some nights—usually Melina and I never found out until the next day—Jan would be called to the hospital to do emergency surgery. She developed a strong dislike for motorcycles, after seeing what these accidents could do to a man's body. Jan and I often had long talks about life. Well, perhaps she didn't talk all that much, but she knew how to listen and she knew how to ask interesting questions. Once—actually, more than once—we were talking about sex and, this time, she said, "I could never surrender to another person." "Jan," I answered, "what has the other person to do with it?"

"Have you any music?" China asked. "I want to dance."

I put on Alan Stivell's *Renaissance of the Celtic Harp*.

"Oh, nice," she sighed, surprised and pleased by the music. I think she expected something not so spiritual. She asked me to light a candle.

What she did next took my breath away.

She stripped off her clothes and danced to the music.

I sat on the bed watching her. China seemed to be in a trance with the Celtic music. She could have been an ancient temple dancer, an incarnation of the beautiful nymph Psyche. I wanted to be here with this woman and only with this woman. China's dark blonde body, the whole meaning of this earth. Her dark blonde body, the wound I carried in my heart. Her dark blonde body, the last dance before the world came to an end. I hardly dared to breathe, hanging by a thread to a feeling of wonder and timelessness. Knowing that the universe had given me a precious gift, as if suddenly the veil between heaven and earth had shifted, and, like the flight of a wild bird going to nest, all I ever wanted danced sweet as a breeze to my door beside the deep woods.

I was a goner, I tell you.

"Dancing is the link between the passing moment and the eternal." I remembered these words from Louis Malle's film, *Phantom India*. Was this the dance of Shiva before me? China had seemed so out-of-place in a bar. She had seemed so mysterious, aloof, and desirable; yet she had done nothing bizarre or strange or glamorous to call attention to herself. She had been wearing a blouse and simple long skirt and shoes with flat heels. She had even seemed a little old-fashioned.

"I want to touch you," I whispered.

She came close to me and I kissed her belly.

I held her for a moment, resting my face on her warm flat belly. I felt her body shiver as my lips touched below her belly. Delicately, I tasted her with the tip of my tongue. She pulled away to lie down on the bed. She lay there for a long time as I hungrily kissed her sweet, wet, gorgeous flower. Finally, she reached for my hands and pulled my mouth to her mouth. She wrapped her legs around me and we danced another dance, as if the world had never ended.

The mystery of attraction continues

We were sitting in the sand on the banks of the Columbia River on the Washington side, idly watching sail boats go by and the seaplanes flying over the water, and people walking up and down the beach. The two of us kept darting like deep-water fish through the undercurrents of the party and our weekend together, and then I watched the sun begin to slide down towards the river in the far distance as I listened to her drift into regions of her memory, growing up in Arizona.

"My body memorized your hands, did you know that?"

I smiled, remembering.

We had left the party around midnight and went to her apartment. Her grandmother was keeping her little girl that night.

"I want you to stay," China said. "But I don't feel like making love."

We curled up together and slept late into Sunday morning.

She got out of bed and then came back with two cups of tea. She put on a tape. I recognized Chopin's *Nocturnes*. She had slipped on an old, faded blue robe when she got up to go into the kitchen. "One day, when I was living in Phoenix," she said, "after taking a bath, I was lying on my bed masturbating and I happened to look out the window. A man was at the window watching me."

I rubbed her shoulders through the robe.

"Hmmm...that feels good."

"I took lessons," I said, proudly. "From my friend, Merika. She's a masseuse. I talked her into getting a group together. We met once a week in her place for two months."

"Right here," she said, pointing to a spot near the base of her spine.

"Ah, yes," I said, knowingly. "Merika says that's a favorite spot for women to hold in energy."

She slipped out of her blue robe.

She allowed my hands to gently loosen the knot at the base of her spine, a splotch of skin turning scarlet. I worked my fingers up her back and into her blonde hair, massaging her skull and the back of her neck, and then down her shoulders and arms and fingers. I kneaded her

178

butt, like kneading bread dough, slipping my hands deep to touch warmness inside her thighs, and then slowly pressed my fingers down the back of her long legs to her feet and toes.

She rolled over.

"You're good at what you do," she said, her eyes smiling at me.

She pulled my hands to her lips and kissed them.

"You have such large hands. They're beautiful. They're like—." She grinned down at my stiff maleness. She looked at my slip of a body and murmured, "Who would have thought?"

We looked into each other's eyes. We both grinned.

She reached down and invited me into her.

China grew up in Arizona with two sisters. All three of them went to college and majored in psychology. (China would have chosen forestry, but at the time—in the mid 1970s—this didn't seem like an option for her. A girl from the desert living in the forest? Her father certainly didn't want her to become a Forest Ranger.) After college, China met a guy in Phoenix who worked as a chef at a popular, highly-rated restaurant. They had a child together. She learned a lot about fancy cuisine and French wine, but when he started dealing coke, and people were coming into their home all hours of the night, she packed her suitcase and took her little girl and moved to Oregon to be near her mother and grandmother.

The gift of spirit traveling had returned to her, she told me. Her older sister called her a shaman and sent her the book *Woman Who Run With Wolves*. Her older sister was now teaching psychology at a university back East. China didn't know about shamans. She simply enjoyed her flying journeys—her journeys, as she called them, "on wings of wonder." Just the same, China wanted to know: "Am I crazy?"

We were having lunch at Café Du Berry.

Over a glass of French wine she said, "I'm a free spirit."

What did she mean by that?

Did she feel scared of losing herself? Of giving up the past? I certainly felt that fear within me. I felt ready at the drop of a hat to give

179

myself away. To take off with her and her little girl to Arizona or anywhere she might want to go. Just like I had always done before with a woman. "You give until there's nothing left and then the woman walks away," a close friend had told me. I knew I had come into China's life at a difficult time. But I knew she liked how I could see into her deep thoughts. She liked being respected and appreciated by a man, something she wasn't used to. She had let her guard down. So here I am, knocking on the door of a great darkness. Empty-handed, I stand at the threshold. I shuffle my feet in fear. I cannot touch this darkness with my hands; cannot grasp it with my mind. I want to embrace this dark beauty with my heart. Will She welcome me? Will She devour me and spit out my bones? As Kali has been known to do to Her devotees.

"Boy, we could never live together," I said, thinking about our differences. To begin with, she was twenty-seven and I was forty-two. I had been married and divorced twice. I wasn't good with kids. Hell, I wasn't even that good with dogs. Not that dogs didn't like me. They did. I just wasn't good with anything I couldn't reason with. Too impatient, I suppose. (All that taking care of....) China felt like an oasis for me, an island paradise, but not the mainland. I wanted stability in my life. I wanted to be with someone who felt as familiar to me as my own thoughts. In other words, I wanted to go home. I wanted to understand how, in the past, I could have loved so deeply and yet have two marriages dissolve into thin air without even knowing what the hell was going on. I wanted to untie the Gordian knot: "Who m I?"

"Why not?" she asked.

She waited for my answer, but I didn't say anything.

Perhaps I had only been fishing.

We sat in silence a few moments.

In fact, emotionally, she reminded me of Naomi.

Suddenly, I felt all this emotion inside me. I actually had to fight back tears. China kept looking curiously at me, her narrow green eyes gauging my face. She reminded me of a cat peering into a mirror. For God's sake, what was she thinking? I could never tell about China. She felt like a free spirit, yes. A free spirit hemmed in a slender body as hot and thirsty as the Arizona desert she came from, and like the desert, she waited for the sudden rain that would bring hidden flowers into bloom overnight.

I wanted to take her clothes off.

She reached over and touched my hand.

Finally, I couldn't hold the words back. "I love you," I said.

"I know," she answered.

We went for a walk. She wanted to smoke a cigarette.

I looked frantically for thick bushes. Or a big tree. Maybe an alley. Any place where we could drop out of sight and I could get her skirt up. China had on a long-sleeved blouse and a dressy, ankle-length skirt and boots. The top two buttons on her blouse were undone and the soft material fell sensually over her shoulders and clung to her shapely breasts. She had trimmed her hair short. She looked sexy as hell. All the time I'd known her, counting the night we met at the bar, I had seen her in a dress only two or three times. She always wore jeans and simple feminine tees or knit polos or jewel-neck blouses without the jewelry. She dressed scantily, even in cool weather. She caught colds easily, she said, and I wondered if it was because of her cigarette smoking or from the way she hardly dressed.

Nothing. I saw nothing to hide us.

She finished her cigarette.

What the hell was I thinking, anyway?

"Thinking, that's good," she said. "To act... I only wish I could."

Not long after our luncheon at Café Du Berry, I had three dreams about China. In one, she wore a dress that belonged to Naomi. I thought that quite odd. Our marriage had lasted six years. And Naomi—like China—almost never wore a dress. My dreams turned increasingly sexual. In the third dream, China and I came that close to making love. Then, suddenly, in the dream, I changed my mind. I woke from the dream, thinking I had made a clear choice. I felt as though I'd been there before. I HAD been there before.

181

I mean, Get serious, David.

Yet, here we were, at happy hour, in an Italian restaurant called Picolo Mondo, drinking Spanish coffees together and talking about our lives and not knowing what to do with our feelings. And then hugging in the parking lot, China pressing her warm body against mine, her kisses stunning me.

"If we don't stop now..." She pulled away, laughing.

I walked to my car in a slight daze. For I really did feel stunned. A very odd feeling. Odd, but certainly not unpleasant; not like anything I could remember. Not an emotional sensation, but a physical one. As if I'd been zapped on the mouth all the way down to my toes. I thought of certain South American natives who put a poisonous plant mixture on the tip of arrows when they hunt spider monkeys, not to kill the monkeys, but to stun and relax the animal's muscles so that the monkey does not cling to the tree and die high up there, but falls to the ground. But that seemed like such a predatory image. Dismiss that thought. And forget the Spanish coffee. Perhaps my friend China did have shamanistic powers, and she had, intentionally or unintentionally, kissed me from her place of power, this coming-into-her-own place of wildness and ferocity and untamed feminine energy deep within her.

In Laura Esquire's book, *Like Water for Chocolate*, the doctor, in part to win Tita's confidence, tells Tita about his grandmother's belief that we are all born with a box of matches inside us. We can't burn all these matches by ourselves. We need each other to light these matches.

And yet—

I don't know if this explains the fire between us. Still, just to think that I still had matches to burn, cheered me greatly. For I have burned a lot of matches. Like the poet Rumi, I have longed for the fire that comes from the Source. And God had come to me time and time again in the breath and heat and presence of a woman. Every woman that I've loved deeply has scorched me to the soul. Has burned away another veil. And I have opened my eyes continuously in wonder to the wisdom of the heart. So, I must have been born with a box chocked full of matches. Better matches, I thought, than chocolates. (But it's a close call.)

So what to do?

She didn't need rescuing.

That's not what China wanted.

She wanted to be free. She wanted to live alone with her daughter. That didn't mean, China assured me, I wouldn't be a part of her life. So she made plans. Practical plans. For she was a practical woman. Perhaps that's why she was fascinated by my passion. And I lived passionately, she told me, and she wanted to be close to that passion, to be a part of that passion. But not just now; now wasn't the time. She had other obligations. Her little girl. A dying mother she loved, who needed her.

Then I had another dream.

In this dream, I went to see a teacher, a well-known spiritual guru. And I met this girl, waiting alone in the darshan line. I call her a girl for she seemed youngish, not quite able to focus on spirit; her awareness fluttered, her energy flickered, like a butterfly. Yet I found myself drawn to her. And she to me. But should I get involved with her? She felt so un-here. Together we went in to see the teacher. We each had written a question and placed them in envelopes, and I put our two envelopes on the pillow before the teacher. He seemed amused by my confusion. He chuckled, and, without opening the envelopes, he answered my question. "Sometimes," he said, "it's necessary to make these loops. People think the spiritual path is easy. They come to a teacher for the answer." He laughed joyfully. "But then," he said, "they have to make the most difficult decisions of their lives."

Take care of your mother, I told China. Take care of your daughter.

Take care of yourself.

Then we'll see.

Yet, if China came near, I wavered, like the girl in my dream. Like an actor in search of direction. So, we stopped writing to each other. We stopped phoning. We kept our distances. We looked at our options, internally circling, like Coyote.

In the teachings of Coyote, Alora told me, life's journey doesn't travel in a straight line, but is circular, and so you can't leave parts of yourself "behind."

"If you have a goal, a desire," Coyote says, "don't approach it directly. Approach in a circular movement. Circle your goal. See its darkness. See its light. See it all. Then sniff it. If it smells good go you, wag your tail. If you can wag your tail, then approach and lie down next to it." But neither of us could "wag" our tails. Certainly I couldn't. In spite of her whispers that she loved me, in spite of her assurance, my doubt would not go away, no more than my desire would go away, no more than the moon would stay forever hidden behind clouds.

I wanted to journey into the darkness. Yet, I had no interest in the darkness called violence, or in the darkness called limitation, or in the darkness called evil—predators that feed upon each other. The best definition of evil I know came from my friend Alora. "Evil," she told me, "is that which does not comprehend or honor the interrelationship between all things. Evil is that which does not consider consequences." I'm not talking demons or angels. The angels do not, and cannot know this dark energy called the human soul. I'm talking the wound of love. I'm talking this earth. I'm talking the unhealed split within us.

I sense two great sides to this darkness within us: a part that nourishes, that regenerates, as the darkness of the earth nourishes the seed, as the womb nourishes the child, as lovers hold hands in the dark. These are hidden places, as the sun in the day hides the light of the stars. Yes, there exists another immense part that holds all our terror and fear and shame: those places of unclaimed power, those places of remorse and regret and sadness, those places that belong to the wholeness I AM.

After years of undoing the darkness within me, to the point that I could calmly say to the universe: "Yes, I want to know this darkness," I thought my direction would take me, like Percival, just down the road a little way, where I'd hang a left and cross the drawbridge and the Fisher King would welcome me to stay for the night as a guest, where we'd swap stories and drink wine, you know, the way good friends do when they haven't seen each other in a long time.

I did not know going into the darkness would bring up all the bittersweet memories of Naomi—memories that would eventually take me all the way back to my mother and the buried rage I felt against her God. I remember, not long after Naomi and I got together as lovers, looking into her "devilish, angelic" eyes and thinking, *If I could reveal your secrets and how you play, but who would believe darkness and light are one?*

Now, perhaps, I understood this. As the Buddhists teach: Start where you are.

I wanted a grand adventure, not a quiet and sobering look into the many ways I had failed to love. I didn't want to relive those memories. I felt finished with the past. It's in the basement, along with old issue of *Rolling Stones* (the one with Bob Dylan interviews) and letters from Jamie Brown, a bunch of old photographs, a poster that says DON'T LOOK BACK, and a framed quote from a Jane Robert's book, something Seth wanted us to know: "*We are all travelers, whatever our position, and as one traveler to another, I salute you.*"

At first, I thought that China might guide me into the interior regions of my being. I thought she might, in her own darkness, in her own journey, accompany me into mine. That, holding hands in the dark, we might comfort each other in our journey. That together, we might explore the shadows we live in, like the mesmerizing shadows in Krzyastof Kieslowski's beautiful film *RED*. I thought eventually we would come to a clearing and behold each other in full moonlight. Warts and all; beauty and all. That we might welcome the new morning together. Yet, strangely enough, I could not romanticize her, nor our situation. Nor could I dismiss the passion between us. So we stopped. Just like that.

Like a painting left undone.

§

**from *Going into the darkness / Tales of past times*
(an unpublished novel)**

This something-in-movement
Or,
CrazyMan Returns to Mother's Arms

1987-1995

§

Every road leads to paradise

*"Roundabouts," says the Centaur. "There is never any
other way."*
—James Branch Cabell, *Jurgen*

In the teachings of Coyote, life's journey doesn't travel in a straight line, but is circular, and so you can't leave parts of yourself 'behind.' "If you have a goal, a desire," Coyote says, "don't approach it directly. Approach in a circular movement. Circle your goal. See its darkness. See its light. See it all...." Henry Miller, I suppose, had something like these words in mind when, in his essay, "Reflections on Writing," he wrote: "Paradise is everywhere and every road, if one continues along it far enough, leads to it. One can only go forward by going backward and then sideways and then up and then down. There is no progress; there is perpetual movement, displacement, which is circular, spiral, endless. Every man has his own destiny: the only imperative is to follow it, to accept it no matter where it leads him."

In 1987, my own destiny lead me to Grand Junction, Colorado. Seven years had passed since Naomi and I had split. Seven years of anger and silence and distance between us, and, for her, a daughter by the man she had left with. For me, seven years of reconstruction; seven years of dismantling old beliefs and false images and self-destructive ideas.

Every seven years, they say, we have a new skin, that all our skin cells have been renewed. For me, this renewal took place in my heart and mind and in the invisible world I live in, as well as in my skin.

Then one day, Naomi wrote me a letter.

She was living alone with her little girl in Colorado.

She wanted to see me.

I called Naomi from some place in Utah, about a hundred miles from Grand Junction. Before I reached the Colorado line, however, I stopped alongside the road and parked my car. I was still driving the 1978 Toyota wagon I had bought a few months after Naomi and I split up. I got out and climbed a tall hill that bordered the road. It was a beautifully clear night with an almost full moon. Living in the city, you can easily forget the night sky, the moon, the stars. For myself, it's like being without a woman for a long time. And when you find each other again, you and this woman, and she opens her arms to you and allows you inside her, in that moment you remember just how exquisitely alive everything is.

I quickly scanned the rocky ground. I reached down and picked up a small, brownish flat stone. I pressed the stone into my palm, storing in the rock my feelings and memories of this place and time. I put the stone in my pocket, got back into my car, and drove on to Grand Junction. I called Naomi again, this time from a pay phone just around the corner from where she was living.

She and her little girl, both barefooted, came running to meet me. I had never seen her little girl before. Alyssa was five years old.

Had Naomi ever looked so fine, so good to me?

We hugged each other on the sidewalk. I took her into my arms, her body warm and lean and sexy as ever in her tight blue jeans, her dark hair all curls tumbling over her forehead and around her shoulders. Naomi had such a pretty face. Such dark, warm, almond-shaped eyes and picture-perfect teeth and sweet, delicately curved lips. I had always loved her mouth. Even when Naomi snarled, she snarled like a wild, beautiful animal.

"I thought you'd get here tomorrow," she said, her statement more a question than a fact. Her voice sounded different from what I remembered when we were together. Not as soft, but plainer, more countrified. More like Colorado.

"I didn't stop much," I said, wondering if I had made a mistake, if I had rushed this meeting, if perhaps I should find some other place to stay for the night.

"No," she said. "I didn't mean it that way."

Then she smiled, looking down at the ground.

"Nice boots," she said.

I had on Apache style lace-up moccasins that came halfway to my knees. They were handmade from soft buffalo hide with six elk horn buttons. I had ordered them earlier in the summer from a boot maker at the Oregon County Fair.

Strange, how much anger Naomi had shown toward me all those years since we split up, and now she seemed so glad to see me, as if we had never quarreled, as if she had never spoken such bitter and humiliating words to me.

At the time, I did not understand her rage.

Sure, I had done stupid things. But nothing, I thought, to have such anger and blame, so much bitterness heaped upon me. Such loss of trust. Such disappointment.

Certainly I had disappointed her.

The child she wanted I did not give her. She must have felt my lack of total fire and enthusiasm, even as we went through all the steps we could possibly take.

Then, one day, she just gave up.

She piled all the baby clothes she had been saving and stuffed them in sacks and gave them to Goodwill. I probably lost her that day and I lost her again the night she went to another man, a friend of mine.

But most of all, I lost her because, as they say, once you break an egg, you can't put it back together again. And we broke the egg, the vulnerable seed called Our Marriage, the thin-shelled, idealized structure that surrounded us, both of us. We broke it deliberately, crazily, painfully.

Naomi liked marriage. She liked her role as a wife. I didn't understand roles. I didn't know the hidden rules. How things worked. I did know, however, that who you are and what you do must come from the center of your being.

But I played hide-and-seek with my heart.

I had no real intimacy with who I am. In fact, I can't recall ever using the word intimacy before my life with Naomi. She intuitively desired true intimacy. Yet, at the age of fourteen, she had been betrayed by a man, a friend of her mother's, and now she approached natural intimacy with suspicion and fear, while I approached with carelessness and fear. Time and time again, I betrayed the natural intimacy between us in small insensitive ways.

"A sticky ball of string," Mala, a spiritual seer, had called our marriage.

"Get a divorce," Mala had told us. That scared the hell out of Naomi. I just shrugged off Mala's warning. I couldn't admit my fear, not to Naomi, not even to myself. For I knew Mala was right. She didn't mean a legal divorce, she meant to undo the darkness between us. She meant for us to unwind the sticky strings, to trace them back to their source, to heal the ancient wounds we carried within us, that we might heal the wounds between us. She meant to open the windows to let clear, fresh air into the house.

"You're choking yourself, David."

Mala told me that. And I knew it. I kept silent out of fear. Fear of Naomi's anger. Fear of her silent withdrawals. Fear of losing her. I could not talk about these feelings. I stuffed them, I swallowed them, I choked on them. I thought the passion between us—between Naomi and me—would make everything all right. I thought the fire between us—Oh, how warmly this fire did burn!—I thought this fire would end my great curiosity about women and put an end to my hunger and desire. My hunger for connection; my desire for wholeness. I thought this fire would burn away the dross of our everyday lives and transform the contents of our everyday lives. I thought the fire between us would burn until our bodies, together in dying, turned to ashes and then blazed even more brightly on the other side.

I thought the fire between us would never die.

Never.

"You want a cup of coffee?" Naomi asked me. "I have French Roast."

My favorite. "Sure."

I had not forgotten how good she was in the kitchen.

Nor would I ever forget that time in her kitchen, back in the summer of 1975, the morning we first became lovers. She was twenty-seven; I was thirty-three. I stood in her kitchen holding a tea kettle, my back to her, my hands shaking, wanting her so much that I couldn't even set the tea kettle on the burner to boil water. She slept upstairs with her husband Marcus; I slept alone downstairs.

192

The day before, in an old stuffed chair in her living room, we had kissed each other for the first time. We broke away and I walked outside. I walked down to the garden near the edge of the woods.

Funny how her kisses disappeared on my lips. They seemed not to leave any memory. I puzzled over this as I stood in Naomi's vegetable garden. I walked back to the house. I made a cup of tea. I mentioned this to Naomi. About her kisses. She understood; I didn't.

She had not kissed me with her whole heart.

She knew that if she did, if she gave me her heart, she wouldn't turn back. She would leave her marriage. She knew she would hurt her husband terribly, her best friend for so many years, and mine since childhood. She knew she would be stepping out into the unknown. If she fell, would I be there to catch her?

It wasn't the breakup of my marriage to Angelina, coming on the heels of our return from living in Europe, but another woman who had acted as the bridge between Naomi and myself. A woman who put Naomi in such a jealous state that she threatened to burn all my writings on Greece and smash my typewriter.

"What's that slut got that I ain't got?" she raged at her husband at two in the morning. Marcus patiently reminded her that she had always acted this way toward my women. "That bastard runs his hand up her bathrobe right in front of me, I could kill him."

I had been friends with Anna Sylvan for a long time and when I first went to see her, not long after Angelina and I came back from Europe and split up our marriage, Anna was living in a rent-free house out in the country near Molalla, with her four-year-old daughter, a child from her off-again, on-again relationship with Eden Maldek. She and her daughter were raising rabbits to eat and sell. Actually, they had only five or six rabbits. But they had a goat. And the house didn't leak. It wasn't quite finished on the inside, but Anna had a double Virgo's touch when it came to delicacy and grace. The day I saw her, she was wearing faded jeans and a shirt unbuttoned at the top and a lavender headband around her auburn hair, which fell way down her back in cascades of light and shadow. With her dark, sad eyes, and her unpainted lips, soft as a primrose, Anna looked every bit a hippie princess in her long dresses and leather sandals and flowers in her hair. I knew that men couldn't resist her. I knew she drove Eden Maldek crazy, by disappearing for days without saying a word. That really didn't concern me. Something else concerned me. I could feel a wound of exquisite pain deep inside Anna. And I had no desire to bring any more pain to her.

The next time I saw Anna, it was July and the temperature was in the nineties. She had moved into Portland and was staying in the guest house that belonged to an old boyfriend of hers. I arrived in the middle of the day and Anna and her daughter were in bathing suits, sunning themselves by the swimming pool in back of the main house. I joined them in a swim.

Anna soon went to make lunch for us, and her daughter wanted me to play make-believe games with her. Monica had just gotten over the chicken pox. Except for Anna, she had been without company for days and she talked my ear off as she imagined adventures for us to act out.

We ate lunch and then Monica went down for a nap.

Toweling dry her long hair after a shower, Anna stood naked in front of the full-length mirror in her bathroom, the bathroom door causally open so that she could talk to me. She kept her voice low as she talked. I sat still as a mouse on her bed. As always, Anna's voice enchanted me. I hardly heard what she said, I felt so lulled by the smoky sound of her voice and her slow, lazy sensuality.

Without any fanfare Anna packed a few things into an overnight bag and went with me out to the country, taking Monica with her. Anna surprised me. Rather than fire, I felt softness. I seemed to sink forever and forever into her gorgeous, frightening softness. I was afraid I might lose myself in the sensuality of her body and in the softness of her voice, and that I might never find my way out.

Did my friend seem a little world weary?

"Nothing surprises me anymore," she said matter-of-factly.

I realized that she was feeling a little sore in places, too.

194

"I'm not used to all this lovemaking," she murmured.

Anna and her daughter stayed three days. Anna had a weeklong camping trip planned with some man, a friend, a lover, she didn't say. She had promised to go with him, and didn't want to break her promise.

I borrowed Naomi's car and drove Anna and her daughter back into Portland. A month passed before I heard from Anna again. By that time, everything had changed.

Three days now, and they were sleeping together in his bed and probably fucking all night, Naomi told herself, and David sure wasn't writing on his book. Anna had even less ambition than herself, if that was possible.

"That inconsiderate bastard!" she raged at Marcus. "He didn't bring my car back. Not that we needed it, but—."

Two days later, when Naomi told me all this, I was stunned. Why was she doing this? What did she want? A fire I had battled to keep down for years, suddenly flamed into new life. I remembered a dream I'd had while in jail in Greece. I had dreamed about Naomi the night after a letter came from her. It was the only letter I got from her during the two years I was in prison for growing hashish plants in a friend's garden. She didn't say much in her letter, but she did send me a bunch of color photographs of her and the house in the country that she and Marcus had bought. That night, in my dream, I saw continents come and go like clouds and simply vanish between Naomi and me. We passed through walls with our whole bodies. I reached out with my hands to touch her in the brightness of her being, to touch her heart.

"I thought you had forgotten me," she whispered. "I couldn't express my feelings, that's why I never wrote you. I dreamed of coming to you in prison. Oh, David, I was so afraid. Would I ever see you again? If you never came back, I couldn't live without not seeing you. I would come to you. I would!"

Later, a few days after our talk, Naomi wore short shorts and a skimpy blouse around the house, something I had never seen her do. She wasn't wearing a bra, either. Yet she acted so normal. As if nothing out of the ordinary was going on. I wanted to look the other way. I thought if I could look past her, or around her, but I couldn't focus on anything that wasn't her.

I knew Naomi didn't like to call attention to herself. When she worked at the bank as a loan officer, she wore dresses that were fashionably short and she looked delicious and sensual in them, yet she didn't care about looking sexy. She liked modest, comfortable clothes.

I had to get out of the house. I walked down past the vegetable garden. Behind a jungle of blackberry vines near the creek, I stripped off my clothes. I lay down on a bed of lush, green, unmowed grass. I lay there with (I figured), the biggest hard-on of my life. I imagined Naomi coming down to the creek looking for me and, miraculously, not turning back. I imagined her—. Ah, but who am I kidding? I would have been mortified if she had actually walked up on me.

The next day, alone together in the house, I put my arms around her. Without saying a word, we kissed each other for the first time.

Naomi had to decide for herself.

I could not tell her what to do. How could I? I did not know her mind. Nor her destiny. I knew she greatly valued fidelity, loyalty. I knew she valued marriage. I knew she loved her husband as a best buddy, even if the marriage between them had died. I knew also that she wanted me. I knew this, she knew this, and so did her husband.

So Destiny, like Coyote, kept circling us.

That morning, in her kitchen, the morning we first became lovers, Naomi watched me carefully. She saw me trembling as I fumbled with the tea kettle. She felt something inside her push her towards me. She walked over to the stove. She put her arms around me. She turned her face up to mine and kissed me. I felt her heart beating wildly yes...yes.

I reached down under her knees with one arm, a little clumsily, and lifted her into my arms. She closed her eyes. She held onto my neck as I carried her into my room.

*****

196

At first, in our marriage, I think Naomi felt some competition with me in the kitchen. The kitchen belonged to her. Gradually, I stopped cooking altogether. I worked my day job as camera operator at the print shop; she stayed at home and took care of Scotty, her adopted son with Marcus, and opened a day-care center. We bought a two-story white house in North Portland near Kenton Park. A corner house. Next to our house stood its twin. Both houses had been built in 1910 by two brothers. In our house, the original woodwork had not been painted over—as the woodwork in so many older homes in Portland has been—and we had leaded windows and a fireplace. (Naomi, I don't think, would ever want to live in a house that didn't have a fireplace.) A wooden front porch and railing ran the full length of the west side. Huge horse chestnut trees lined both sidewalks.

With Naomi as architect and chief carpenter, we built a white picket fence around our small, mostly shaded backyard. I put in a tiny lawn for Scotty to play on, and we grew our vegetables in a community garden. We had carpet installed in the living and dining rooms (the floors weren't hardwood), and Naomi set in to remodeling the kitchen. Day after day in the summertime, she worked long hours preserving peaches and strawberries and green beans and corn. (The best way to get rid of a million fruit flies, I found out, is to use a vacuum cleaner.)

Naomi wanted a dog, and so we got a little Boston Terrier named Betty Boop. Boopsie loved everyone, and without a second thought, she would trot off down the sidewalk after a stranger. We only had her for a short time. She escaped the backyard one evening and got killed by a car, even as I was working on the picket fence to make it higher, so that she couldn't scramble over it.

Naomi loved to go camping. She loved to travel, sleep in a tent, cook outdoors. We took camping trips to the Oregon coast and to Crater Lake. The Jedediah Smith Redwoods State Park in northern California became our favorite vacation spot. As you can see, a traditional marriage gradually formed around us. *The full catastrophe,* as Zobra called it.

And then, as if overnight, everything came undone. In Grand Junction, in Naomi's tiny kitchen, we had coffee together for the first time in seven years. Later, after Alyssa had gone to bed in her own bedroom, we talked until two.

"You want me to sleep on the couch or outside?" I asked. By outside, I meant the small mobile home parked in back. The mobile home belonged to her mother. Her mother lived a few miles away on a ranch with one of Naomi's brothers.

"What do you want?" Naomi asked.

"I'd rather sleep here."

She disappeared into her bedroom and I rolled out my sleeping bag on the couch. I crawled into my bag just as she came back into the room. She had changed from her shirt and jeans into a thin nightgown.

"I'm not sleepy," she said.

She sat down in the ragged, overstuffed chair next to the couch and pulled her knees up to her chest, hugging them. Strange, how relaxed and safe I felt with her. I couldn't feel a trace of her old anger, not a hint of blame. We didn't even talk about it.

In the letter Naomi sent me, she had written about going to Adult Children of Alcoholic Parents. Her anger, she realized, had little to do with me. She wanted to acknowledge this. And she had been thinking of a Seth book by Jane Roberts she knew I had. She wanted to read the book. I called her on the phone and we talked for a long time. I made plans to go to Colorado. She wrote me another letter. She told me about a dream she had. She dreamed of a stream of light entering her and she knew that this stream of light was me. I did not tell Naomi, but I knew her dream had been more than a dream. At least, more than an ordinary dream. I didn't want to tell her for I was afraid she might get scared. Then she called me on the phone and said she had decided to move back to Portland at the end of September, which was three weeks away. But I didn't want to wait. I wanted to see her in Colorado.

We looked at each other. She smiled.

I had changed, she had changed. All the way to Colorado, I couldn't help but wonder, What if? I would not know until the moment we saw each other. I knew how easily one moment goes into its opposite. One moment you're a hero, the next a goat.

Desire flickers this way, that way.

I knew Naomi did not easily change her feelings. Casual sex? Forget it. Naomi belonged to the earth, to trees, to rocks, to home and hearth. She could build a fence, a wall, a home. She loved fires, and between us, I realized, the fire had not died, not yet.

God, how much I wanted her. As I had always wanted her. How long ago since that night in San Francisco? Almost twenty years. Almost that night we had crossed the line. Before Angelina. Before Greece. Before prison.

I got out of my sleeping bag.

I moved over to her chair.

She looked at me, her eyes unwavering.

I raised the edge of her nightgown. She opened her legs slightly. I tasted her. Moist. Yummy and sweet. Of all women, Naomi tasted the sweetest.

She took me by the hand and I followed her.

Epilogue

David and Naomi's second time around didn't last long.

Naomi returned to Portland with Alyssa and rented a house in SE Portland. Naomi claimed that Eden came to the house only to see their daughter. She wasn't, she claimed, having sex with Eden. David quickly found out that wasn't true.

Without trust, once more, their lives went separate ways.

Paradise lay farther down the road.

Much farther, as David found out.

Years later, after all the debris from the wreckage of their marriage had floated downstream, once more they could acknowledge the deep love they felt for each. Not as romance, but as an abiding spiritual connection crossing over many lifetimes. Naomi was now happily married. Alyssa had grown into a young woman. Scotty traveled back and forth between Portland and Alaska. Marcus and Carolyn now lived in the South. After David and Alora split up, during the time of the

199

"harmonic convergence," he bought a house, then lived alone for the next fifteen years and tended the cottage garden he had so lovingly created. Then he met the woman he would spend the rest of his life with, whatever that might bring, wherever that might take them.

§

**from *Going into the darkness / Tales of past times*
(an unpublished novel)**

This something-in-movement

To reach into the fire,
To bring the burning into words;
To enter the darkness,
To remember —
    David Pendarus
    — "The Burning"

You came to me
through a handful of light,
a mere cluster of stars—
like soft yellow flowers
in a room of white.

You called to me
and I answered your call;
or was it I
who called to you?

I remember a desert,
a great burning distance,
a caravan of illusions
passing like rain between us;
and I remember mountains, bitter
as the betrayal of a brother,
not knowing if I would ever see you
or if I was simply dreaming;
and I remember walking in the ruins
of great cities,
down streets diseased, overrun
with neglect and the crying
of children.

And they say I went crazy,
that I cursed the Mother
Of All Living Things;
that I tore out my heart
and made war on the Earth.
And they say that you built a great wall
out of fear, out of anger and jealousy,
high as a cathedral around you,
and that you never came out,
a long time ago.

*****

*It was such a cold winter I remember. At times,
the chill numbed me to its destructiveness; mostly
though, it caused pain, sharp and biting. I lost
several fingers to frostbite, and a toe as well.
And the storm froze one dear one to death.*

*Even now it brings me pain and fear, the memory
does. No way would I ever choose to live through,
or even try to survive, such a lonesome freeze ever again.*

*But you remind me that these are memories,
real enough to grip my bones and make me shiver.
Yet merely memories, nonetheless.*

*To tell my story, though, helps me, my brother.
The elders know this. Their storytelling is for
instruction, a passing on of wisdom. However, it is
also so clearly a means to validate their experiences
and a way to make sense of the pain.*

Those fierce and unpredictable winds burned my
face and rubbed my soul raw. The winter was real
with a vengeance.

And now here, by the fire with you, the telling
of my tale softens the sorrow, begins to heal
the cold knifelike pain that lingers within me.

*****

But most of all,
I remember how you turned to me,
in a garden called choice,
the light dancing around us,
and not even the meadow grasses
in fields of white clouds,
or even the thoughts of angels,
could know such tenderness as the love
we felt between us,
our hearts one with all that is,
and we made this covenant,
each to each—
before the beginning,
before sorrow and pain and self-doubt;
before our journey into loss and separation—
a sacred pledge
that we would never forget,
that not even ten thousand deaths
or all the darkness in the world
could overshadow: this
moment:
this love:
this something-in-movement
that calls me to you.

Grace & grit

A time too soon,
I shall not walk this lovely green earth
again, nor see the radiant sun break,
nor feel the breeze sudden spring blows
across my face; nor touch once more
this woman whom I have loved;
this woman whose eyes dazed mine
with brightness, whose glance nestled
my heart in folds of sleepless love.
    —David Pendarus, *A Time Too Soon*

Years ago, we had been lovers and now she was dying. She was dying of cancer. I had not seen Aditi in months, and, when an invitation came to a Christmas party at her house, I made plans to go. From Merika, I learned that Aditi had moved in with a woman named Viola. Viola, I gathered, was an artist, a painter, but I had never met her. During this 1993 Christmas season, Aditi played more than thirty performances of the *Nutcracker Suite* for the Seattle Symphony. Aditi played the bass. At one time, she had been rated among the top ten bass players in the United States. That was before she stopped playing, before she went to India, before she gave up everything to become a follower of Bhagwan Shree Rajneesh.

She liked the way I danced. That's the reason she went home with me, she liked the way I danced, she said, that first time we met in the spring of 1981, over twelve years ago, at one of Mala's emotional-energy workshops. I had not instantly liked her though, I can tell you that. I was a little put off by her. She seemed judgmental and very needy. Nor did I feel attracted to her physically. She was tall, large-boned, full breasted, kind of lanky. She had dark, straight hair and she didn't shave her legs. She smiled a beauty of a smile though. Her warm dark eyes, her full mouth, her whole face lit up when she smiled. Her smile came from one of the kindest hearts I've ever known.

I had just gone through a sudden, painful divorce.

204

I felt lost, bewildered. Our split-up had happened so fast. Like the snapping of a branch. Like one moment you're driving along in your car dreaming of how your wife looked last night, how she felt so sweet in your arms, so much in love with you and then, suddenly, another car weaves out of nowhere, crossing the line head-on into your path.

Only it's not a dream, this car.

So I was glad to dance with Aditi. Glad she went home with me.

We soon drifted apart, however. A sannyasin, a Bhagwan devotee, a wearer of orange, I would never be. I enjoyed reading Bhagwan's books and listening to his taped discourses. I did his kundalini meditation for months and went to a number of workshops facilitated by Mala and Aniruddha, sannyasins who had recently returned from his ashram in India. I felt his grand love and his magnetic pull. Yet I felt no push from within to become a follower. Maybe, as Angelina would say, I was just too independent.

When Bhagwan came to the United States and established his spiritual community at Antelope in eastern Oregon, Aditi moved to the Rajneesh Ranch. I drove out a few times to visit her, but I didn't feel comfortable in such an organized state of watchfulness. I felt watched all the time. And not as a mother duck might watch her ducklings out of concern. The Ranch energy felt intimidating and too paranoid.

Now and then, whenever Aditi came back to Portland, we'd see each other. Sometimes she worked at the Rajneesh Hotel on SW Eleventh. Aditi always wondered who would be the lucky woman to end up with me. Anyway, that's how she put it.

When the Ranch escalated into full-blown paranoia with armed guards protecting Bhagwan, and when Sheila, the Duchess Dowager of the whole shebang, tried to take control and drive out or poison her rivals, and when she even, so the story goes, tried to kill Bhagwan, and Bhagwan, with a few chosen ones, attempted to flee the country by private jet but was nabbed and jailed in North Carolina and charged with immigration fraud and, after agreeing to a plea bargain, was banished from the United States, and the Ranch closed, Aditi stayed on until everything that could be sold was sold, including the peacocks.

She went to Boston and took an apprenticeship as an electrician. Then she moved to a small town near San Francisco and did her electrical work and studied herbal medicine and developed a passion for good wine. She drifted into a relationship with a man she worked with, a married man, and the whole thing left her feeling frustrated and disappointed.

Aditi decided to play music again. She moved back to Oregon.

A year after coming back to Portland, Aditi found out she had cancer. With Merika and her husband, Odell, I went to see her in the hospital. A surgeon had removed one of her kidneys. They had gotten all the cancer. Or so they thought.

A year and a half later, she's undergoing radiation treatments, but not the really heavy-duty chemotherapy kind Treya Wilber underwent for her breast cancer in Ken Wilber's book *Grace and Grit*. Aditi had read *Grace and Grit* several times by the time I saw her at the Christmas party.

Aditi and I were squeezed together in a big comfy chair. It was still early in the evening but already she seemed exhausted. She had barely touched her glass of wine. She must have been in pain but she kept smiling.

"Viola, I want you to meet David. He's the man I've talked so much about."

Viola had a soft, breathless voice.

In a few minutes, she drifted away.

Aditi must have read my mind.

"She chose the name Viola for herself," she said. "Her spirit name."

I nodded. "How old is Viola?"

Aditi called her back.

"I'm thirty-four."

Viola was wearing a multi-colored, patch-quilt jacket Aditi had made for her as a Christmas gift and she had on tight black pants and slim black boots and a brimmed burgundy felt hat. A tall, slender woman with dark hair and a pretty face, I could easily have taken her for Aditi's sister. As I remember, I fell in love with her hat. And the way she kind of sloughed through the crowd and smiled warmly at everyone, as if she were a guest at her own party, rather than the host, anxious to take care of everyone.

My imagination fluttered.

I had no shame. My friend was dying and I was thinking of romance.

Across the room, Viola smiled at the two of us.

Viola's paintings hung on all the walls around us. Large, strange paintings of women in pain. Paintings of a woman who identified with the wolf, the bird, the shaman, the artist. The one that held my eye the most was a thick, heavy-painted, layered portrait of a child-woman emerging from pain, and all this shit flying in the air around her.

I learned that Viola had just finished two years of intense psychotherapy. She had come out of a painful, dreadful darkness that went back into childhood horrors, into sexually abusive events so shameful to her that she had split herself into multiple personalities.

I knew little about multiple personality disorder.

I knew about splitting-off in my own self. Indeed, I knew about that. But I didn't know the depths that one might take this splitting, to distance oneself from the pain, from the humiliation, from the powerlessness. And then to have the courage, the guts, the grit, to find one's way out of this darkness into the light; to come out of this wounded place screaming; to come out of this living death alive.

At the Christmas party, with Aditi's family and Viola and other close friends in the same room—especially Odell and Merika, close friends of mine, too—and Roberto, a handsome, dark-haired man who wrote music and wonderful poetry, and his lovely wife, Kathy, who played violin in the Oregon Symphony—I suddenly realized the truth that Aditi would be leaving us soon.

We sat together, the two of us, holding each other. We had come together at the beginning in the place called Heart. Our lives did not mesh, we had different journeys to take, our paths ran parallel and not together, yet in her final days our journeys had come together once again. We could hold each other in this sacred moment, in this place of coming together, without needs, without nervousness, without fear. Quietly, we rested in this place.

§

**from *Going into the darkness / Tales of past times*
(an unpublished novel)**

Wild strawberries

for Sarah (age 28)

Remember how fresh, how sweet, they tasted
in your mouth,
that summer night you came home
with me?
"The berries, they're so juicy," you said.
"So sweet."
You held one in your mouth,
your red-stained mouth,
and you kissed me.
I tasted the wildness in your life,
your reckless youth,
your sadness, your skinny nakedness,
thin as my own.
How could you be so thin,
slender as a flame,
your legs dark spotted with bruises
from falling down
and bumping into corners,
yet so wild, red-stained and delicious?
You smiled at my seriousness,
your dark, blue shaded eyes
catching the curve
of my heart
like a blue Bellflower catching the flight
of a hummingbird.
In another life
We could have been storybook lovers,
husband and wife,
traveling with little money in another country,

Italy, the town of Brindisi,
on the coast,
drinking red wine from a barrel
in a small tavern,
waiting for a boat to Greece.
On the side of the road,
near Sparta,
wild roses ripped at your dress
as you leaned too close
to capture their fragrance,
do you remember?
But that was a long time ago,
this other life.
More than twenty years.
You would have been only eight years old.
I could have been your father,
had I known your mother.
Only I've never had a daughter,
never had a son.
I don't understand time, nor age,
nor this emptiness that I feel
inside my chest.
Time evaporates like kitchen clouds
steaming out of a kettle,
swallows us like fog
on a river bridge,
and disappears like wild strawberries
in your red-stained mouth.
"My heart belongs to another," you said,
"but I will stay with you tonight, if you wish."
I lay without sleeping in the dark,
thinking of you

and of the sacred emptiness of all things,
all night,
tears claiming my heart
as your arm reached out and curled
like the tip of a wave
around me,
an old man in love
with a woman he does not know.

Endless the beginning

1996-2005

§

Endless all that I am,
and endless this journey to you.

Before the beginning

He had no idea where he was or how he got here. He had no memory of any events, no memory of any journey. Perhaps a shipwreck? He knew ships. He had seen one pass by in the watery distance—too far away for him to signal. The big silver birds that flew across the sky, sometimes at night, with lights flashing—could he have fallen from the belly of one of those giant birds? His clothes offered no clues. He had on a long-sleeve flannel shirt, a blue coat with big pockets and a hood, blue denim jeans, athletic shoes. Already the day had warmed and he removed the jacket and his shirt. Inside his coat, in a pocket, he found a worn leather wallet. In the wallet, he found a driver's license, a credit card from a bank, several new twenty-dollar bills, an old, torn library card, a ticket stub to a movie. He felt something else deep inside the coat pocket. He stared curiously at the object—a black and white photograph of a young woman. The woman was smiling warmly into the camera. She had nice teeth and a lovely, relaxed smile, a sensual mouth, and a slight mischievous look in her eyes. The woman had pinned her dark hair behind her head and the wind whipped a few wispy strands of loose hair about her face. In the hazy background, he saw a low, tree-covered mountain, and just beyond the mountain, he could make out a body of water, probably an ocean, like the one now surrounding him. The woman had on a sleeveless blouse and she wore a beaded necklace. The pattern on her blouse seemed to match the design on the large glass beads around her slender neck. The woman, he could tell, possessed a kind heart. Affection and freedom—he saw these in her smile and in her eyes. Hope, time, identity; these all belonged to her. A thin bra strap showed on her right arm, slightly below her shoulder. His eyes lingered on the picture. He had no memory of this beautiful woman.

He studied his driver's license, looking for some clue to the past. He had no idea how many years had passed since the picture on the license was taken, but the picture showed a man obviously younger than himself. He suddenly felt an emptiness inside his belly. He recognized that feeling. He was hungry. An apple. He wanted an apple. But he didn't know the meaning of that word *apple*. He said the word over in his mind several times. Then he saw an image. He saw a roundish, dull golden fruit with a splash of red coloring its skin. Ah, so that's an apple, he thought. And the color red. He liked the word red. But what did the word mean? He felt a current of energy tingle through his body. He bit into the red and dull golden skin of the fruit. Juice ran down his lips. The apple tasted sweet and crisp, as if it had suddenly ripened on the tree. He ate the apple and looked out upon the water around him. He took off his shoes, his socks, and walked barefoot on the sand. The sand seemed to welcome his feet. He had no idea where he was going or how long he walked. A thin, cold stream fed into the sea from a single tributary on the land. He took off his clothes and placed them carefully on the ground. He walked into the sea. Overhead, sea birds watched him curiously. He swam in the water and then washed the salt from his body in the thin, cold stream. He dried himself with his T-shirt. He walked inland, away from the sea.

He sat on a high bluff, out of the wind. He watched the sun go down and thought that he had never seen such a spectacular transformation as the sun vanished over the water and the moon appeared and the stars dotted the night sky. A large, golden moon. Another word that comforted his tongue. He said the word 'moon' several times. How did he know moon? What did this word mean? He sat spellbound, as if he had never seen the night sky before. Perhaps he hadn't. Perhaps the flying ships in the night had all been a dream. How could he fall from such a height and not perish on the rocks or break apart? There had to be another explanation. He dismissed the idea of a shipwreck. His wallet would have been soaked; the picture of the woman would have been damaged. The moon reminded him of the woman. Both were as wondrous and as unknown as anything he knew. Considering his predicament, and how little he knew, he pondered the irony, for he felt absolutely safe. He wondered how that could be. How could he feel safe, alone, not knowing who he was or where he had come from, and certainly not seeing any place to go from here? He cupped the moon in his hands. The woman contained earth, warmth, life; the moon felt cool and indifferent to his presence. He could not warm the moonlight with his hands. He turned his eyes to the stars. The stars both amused and awed him. They twinkled in the sky, like little kids who couldn't sit still and were just waiting to run outside to play. Their great number astounded him. They reached from one end of his out-stretched arm to the other arm and beyond. He couldn't contain all the stars, there were too many. He touched a star very carefully, then another. They looked so far away, and yet all he had to do was reach out with his mind to hold one in his hand. They were beautiful, but he had no desire to be a star. He wanted to be one with the woman; with earth, fire, time. If he could touch the stars, why couldn't he remember this woman? Why couldn't he put himself in her eyes, and touch her spirit with his, and come home to her? Surely, she waited for him, carrying his memory locked in her heart, just as he carried the black and white photograph of her in his pocket. Perhaps this is all a dream he thought: the sea, the land and the flying ships in the night, the stars he could easily touch. Perhaps, he thought, I will awaken and find myself at home in bed, warm and safe with this woman, and she'll be half-smiling in her sleep with her arms wrapped around my chest and her hair slightly tangled across her face. Or perhaps I've gone mad. This idea made him smile. Suddenly, he remembered a poem. It was a poem about a man counting the stars and writing them down on a piece of paper, and everyone thought the man was crazy, or else a genius, for he wanted to protect the stars from the rain, and the man only half-smiled out of one side of his mouth when they questioned him. Of all the poems he had read in his lifetime, strange, he thought, that he should remember this one. But none of this made sense to him. Why should he remember one thing and not another? He touched the stars once again, to make sure they were real. Then he wrapped himself as best he could in his blue coat and, thinking of the woman, he fell into a deep sleep. He dreamed he was coming home.

§

**from *Going into the darkness / Tales of past times*
(an unpublished novel)**

I remember

I came to live my life not by conscious plan or prearranged design
but as someone following the flight of a bird.
—Sir Laurens van der Post

For Jane

Listen to the air around you,
my love.
If you hear shimmering beats
know that I am near,
know that I am calling to you,
"Let's go, let's go!"
Sssh, sssh, my lovely bird,
the night is a long flight.
Here, rest your head on
my breast,
the way lovers do.
Here, close your eyes.
Do you now see the lights
of home?
Do you remember?
Oh… yes… yes!
I remember. I remember.

Outside my thoughts

for Blazek, Kryss, & Willie

Time to get ready "not to be here,"
as a famous poet once wrote in a poem
he wrote one morning in winter,
when ice lay on the ground
and the temperature froze his words
in the north country air above my head.
Time to get ready, he said in his poem;
and I thought: Is that not
the meaning of time, from
the beginning—time to get ready
to go home, to the one you love,
to the lights that never go dark,
to arrive at last to who you are,
with no strings attached.
Outside my thoughts,
a whole universe goes on.

Endless

Endless comes life
in the Spring, in every Spring.
"Away with lullabies,
sad songs, your eyes that close in tears!"
we cry to the flowers;
we beckon the sunbursts
between the quickening showers.

Show me your secrets
and I'll show you mine;
and I'll show you every doubt
the budding rose, the dandelion,
the bumblebee,
will joyfully put out.

Endless goes the cycle,
endless my heart, loving you.
Endless all that I am,
and endless this journey to you.

Looking out my kitchen window at the cemetery

2006-2010

§

Whatever Unknown and Unknowable Spirit there is in the universe, this Spirit has brought forth untold billions of individuals with unique fingerprints and auto-biographies that seem to last no longer than dreams. This unutterably beautiful but often terrifying world we live in is a fact that never ceases to evoke wonder in me, and I must confess I cannot understand it. To me, the agony and the beauty of the human condition is to be eternally and inevitably ignorant of our ultimate origin and destiny.
—Larry Setnosky, in a letter

§

Into this Universe, and Why not knowing
Nor Whence, like water willy-nilly flowing;
And out of it, as wind along the Waste,
I know not Whither, willy-nilly blowing.
—Omar Khayyam, The Rubaiyat

In praise of Basho, W. C. Williams, & Charles Bukowski

This morning,
looking
out
through the kitchen
window,
a cold
January morning,
I saw a deer,
nimbly
walking through
the gravestones
near
the crematorium
in
the cemetery
across
the street
from our house.

How delightful!
I thought.
So much depends upon
this cemetery!

Knowledge on the line
A few questions

With your life on the line,
with a loved one dying,
what book,
what piece of knowledge,
will your draw upon?
What truth
doesn't come from who you are?
Who do you think God
is made of?

"Bless all you see,"
Ramas once said to me,
"and let the world
fall apart,
as you bless it.
Just let go, and love.
Open your heart and love."

Even if I can't carry a tune

An e-mail dialogue with John Bennett
in response to his shard:
THE ROSEY CRUCIFIXION

who the fuck is Cornel West?
and why should I know him?

if you don't know who levy is,
you're cornel west...

if you don't know who cornel west is,
you have transcended
everything
and are god almighty himself...
congratulations, Don!

well, I know levy...
since the 60s.
so I ain't cornel west.
and Jane
(my partner)
will tell you that I'm not god
almighty himself...
close...
but not quite.

then you're the mystery man...

just about everything's a damn mystery to me.

then it's time to take the magical mystery tour...

you got a ticket to ride?

ah, yes, but it's scalped and will cost you...
last seat on the bus
(which you are either on or off...)...

who's driving this bucket of bolts, anyway?
levy's dead. Kesey's dead. Lennon's dead.
even Bukowski, who never liked buses,
he's dead.
what the hell's going on?
who's driving this damn bus?

neal cassady...it was difficult to arrange...

a long pause.

I see.
this is no ordinary bus.. .is it?
destination: unknown.
oh, look, there's Tom Kryss with his rabbits!
sweet Jesus, who's that beautiful woman?
(I'm sure I've seen her somewhere before.)
what a lovely voice she has!
damn, it's 4:28 in the morning.
when do we leave?

shortly.

that's it?
no good-byes from the depths of the soul?
no words of wisdom?
no memories to relive?
no tears of remorse?
no wiseass advice?
no broken hearts?

no reciting of scriptures?
no mumbo jumbo?
no books to carry?
no secrets untold?
no regrets?

no.

we just disappear?
vanish? without a trace?
no collection boxes?
no tombstones?
no ashes?
no shrines along the road?

poof.

you mean, the party's over?
it's closing time?
as in that great Leonard Cohen song?
but, hey, it's a new day, right?
who knows what's around the next bend,
right? or just over the hill?
wait...
I see a glimmer of light.
it must be time.
any last thoughts?

-30-

I see.

I'm on my own...

ok,
a last farewell,
(without being sentimental
or tough; is that not
the hard part?)
to friends… family…
Jane…
("Gone to New Seasons"
she once joked
would be my epitaph)
in this life I have
acted the coward, a thief, a liar,
a poet, a lover, full of pride,
a king (a make believe king,
wearing not a crown of stars
but of cinders),
an outlaw, a prisoner in a foreign land.
a traveler, a mystic, a beginner,
a working stiff, a sanctimonious ass, a fool,
a nice guy,
a family man
(a role, I'll admit,
that didn't suit me well
and that didn't last long).
I have wrestled with angels,
thinking they were demons;
and I have entertained demons,
thinking they were gods.
I've been a seeker after Truth,
only—I'm a slow learner—to discover
I carried this truth within me—
and this is my truth: LOVE—

even as I carry you within me,
and the memory of home
deep within all that I am and am not
like an acorn within a giant oak tree.
simply put,
I am who I am becoming…
a man…
a man who loves.
a jewel of a man.

I leave you
now
with this single thought.
remember this.
this is important.

all those who crave knowledge,
all those who pray and beseech the gods;
all those who stumble and fall along the way,
all those who think there is only one way
to heaven
and those who laugh
at this one true god-forsaken way;
all those who live in fear and those who love
without the help of anything on Earth;
all those who hide their thoughts in the shadows
of tall buildings
and those who look inward for all to see;
all those who would rather be right than real,
and all those who think they are lost
and those who think they have been found;
all those who wish--

oh, damn, the bus...!

I gotta go,
gotta get on this conceit of a bus,
like some Book of the Dead tug boat
crossing the great waters,
or that mythological chariot
with the crazy Greek at the reigns,
charioting me off to the underworld.

there's no bus.
(John made that up.)
no band of angels.

there's only Light...light
everywhere...
and in every cell of my body,
a great singing.

...

with your life on the line,
or a loved one dying,
what book,
what piece of knowledge
will you draw upon?

Don Cauble/ John Bennett

They could not remember a time

for Jane, partner in time

No matter how long I sit and stare
at these freshly painted walls,
or the living plants so rich and green,
or the stars I see through our windows
with their grand view of Mt. St. Helens,
snow-capped in the distance,
or how long I gaze into the light around you,
as you read your book of mysteries,
both of us knowing, in our understanding,
that this too shall pass,
when I think of you,
and wait for my heart to speak,
I am filled, almost overflowing,
with this deep, unfathomable silence.
Words—like these—
seem trivial, almost obscene,
and yet, and yet...
I must give words to this that is:
my heart feels at peace with you in this room
and this deep, unfathomable silence.

An essay in which I attempt to explain to a friend how I see the world

*(Author's Note: Feel free to skip this part of **Book Four** since explanations can not only be boring but are often deceptive and misleading.)*

§

I confess I have trouble reconciling that very spiritual, very mystical, very Zen, radical nondual teaching with my experience of time right here and now. If my watch tells me it's now 3:30 p.m., how can I at the same time be living in eternity?
—Larry Setnosky, in a letter, June 2008

To begin, I'll skip your adjectives like "spiritual, mystical, Zen," and just go with the nondual term. I have no problem with the thought of living at 3:30 p.m. and living in eternity "at the same time." However, I do not define eternity in terms of physical immortality or physical existence or continuation. That would be silly. At least, to my experience. Not that I have some mystical experience or perception of eternity. Or 3:30 p.m. for that matter. They are both thoughts to me. One is a thought-measuring stick—the clock. Plus an awareness of night and day, the earth in relation to the sun, my body rhythms, that sort of thing. The other is more or less a sense of being outside of time...or the limitations of time. I can go with your thought that "I am time," but that doesn't exclude the thought "I am forever." Again, I'm not defining myself here as simply a physical existence or even a mental existence or even a soul existence... but existence itself.

(Actually, I don't much think in terms of "eternity." I much prefer the word "forever.")

Eternal Present. An interesting thought. But basically meaningless. Nor do I think that, in a true sense, we live in the present and, as you say, **"Most of us run away from the present because it is too uncomfortable."** Let me back up. You write about the Buddhist philosophy of relative truth and ultimate truth. I have no idea what ultimate truth is and neither do I think a Buddhist knows what ultimate truth is. Unless, perhaps, they mean by Ultimate Truth: I AM. An example for me is Newton's view of the universe. (An example I've probably used before in our exchanges.) This is a great truth. What goes up comes down, and the earth revolves around the sun, and all those laws we see in action in our physical universe. However, I believe the quantum view of the universe is a greater truth. It does not nullify the Newtonian view of the world but includes and goes deep into the world "where nothing appears to be." To call this the ultimate truth would be way presumptuous on our part. How can we call anything that we think or perceive or experience as the ultimate truth?

A conceptual sleight of hand: to call relative truth the same as absolute truth.

Maybe it is; maybe it isn't.

Our experiences can hardly tell us what's real and what's not real, much less what is absolute truth. To experience anything involves duality, as you well recognize. There's the state of meditation and the "I" who experiences the state of meditation. If the two become one, how are we to know? (Perhaps you suddenly emerge from the state and realize that "you" were not there?) I have no problem with "I" or with the "self" or with "desire" and with a lot of things that the Ancients wanted to dismiss as not being "real." How could they even say the "I" is temporary? By seeing that we die and that we have a temporary presence in this physical world? How does that prove anything other than what it is: we die and have a temporary presence in this world?

As Walt Whitman crows: "I am large. I contain multitudes." He contains the whole of his world. Of his truth. And that world merges with mine even as I write this. Not just in some metaphorical sense but in the sense that we are here, now, forever. This is an inner thought, Larry; or whatever you want to call it. Sure, many would call it "denial." But they have no more proof of their "reality" than I have proof of this feeling, this knowingness, within. Relative truth—absolute truth—lower self—higher self—we can say yes, they are one and the same; they just wear different masks. I like the term "altered self"—this is the self of social consciousness, the self that leaves us feeling empty because, basically, it's a bubble on the ocean (to use a Buddhist metaphor). It's the self we create and forge and put together to live in this world and the self that so many of us come to accept as our true, authentic self. The true, authentic self is the "I" in touch with that-which-can-not-be-named and that-which-eludes-our-thoughts-and-our-philosophies. As in quantum physics, we can only deduce or conclude that this "I" must be there. We cannot experience this "I" because we are this "I" and to experience something, we need a split. We can only be this "I." Still, we go in search of this "I" in the name of enlightenment and all those other grand names we've inherited from the Ancients.

Eternal Present.

I don't experience the "I" that I AM. Neither do I experience the Now. I don't even experience the Present in our normal sense of the word, Larry. I experience, in our normal sense of the word, the immediate past. Perhaps I'm slow, but by the time I perceive something, that event has already come and gone. Yes, this happens so quickly that we think—we assume for all practical purposes—that it's the present. So we're running from the past. Perhaps many would think this is too subtle a distinction of past-present-future. In my ordinary day-to-day life, I certainly distinguish between past and present in the normal sense. But we can certainly fine-tune our perceptions and emotional awareness so that we know when we're dealing with issues from the "past" and when we're dealing with an event in the "here and now." For instance, I know when it's Jane speaking—or maybe Jane's mother or her father—and not *my* mother or *my* father from way back in my memory banks. "It's not the past if you keep dragging it around with you." That's a quote from Polinski, years ago when we were married, and a quote that I still treasure.

The more we live in the "here and now," the closer we approach that feeling of authentic self and to the truth I AM. Trying to catch this self is, to use an ancient metaphor, like trying to grab the tiger by its tail. You can't think fast enough. In other words, you're chasing your own tail.

The sense of lack... the sense of loss...

We could ask: *Where* is this lack? *Where* is this loss?

Certainly, in performance, I lack the ideal of how I want to be and act in this world. The other evening, after I placed Rosie's food tray in the utility room—Rosie, our border collie, is moving really slow these days and she hasn't yet got to the utility room—Milo makes a beeline for Rosie's food—and Milo knows this is not where she gets fed—and I stick out my foot to prevent Milo from going into the utility room. I forgot that I had on flip-flops. Milo chomps down on my foot with her teeth. In an instant, I grab Milo by the throat and throw her halfway across the kitchen floor. This is not the first time Milo has bitten me— her bite didn't draw blood, but I was so mad, so quickly, that my thoughts were filled with rage and the thought of killing that dog. Yep, in the moment Milo's teeth came down on my foot, I experienced the whole world of separation between myself and this other creature. If I did not have such self-control—if I wasn't so rational—my quick trigger reaction might have meant a bad end for Milo. (Something that I would have regretted for sure.) And this "spiritual consciousness" of mine... damn near gone in a flash... so how can I judge another or ride a high horse? Or even consider that I've mastered my emotions or left behind my reptilian brain?

A matter of lack... or a matter of forgetting... or a matter of not remembering... or a matter of ignorance... a genetic imprint... or just bad temper?

Is the lack within us? Or how we perceive ourselves?

Can you identify yourself without a greater social identity?

I think of Buddhism, in this case, as a greater social identity. Like being an American. Or a UO Duck fan. Or a poet. An artist. Jane thinks in terms of family. I think in terms of friendships. I'm comfortable being three thousand miles from my sister and other family members. Yet, I love my sister and we are close. I love my brother, but both of us like our solitude. (A solitude that can have its conflicts with Jane's family needs.) I'm comfortable having a friend such as you living at a distance. (A friend "such as you"... well, I don't have any other friends "such as you.") Even my wonderful friend Michael, we can talk about anything, the way you and I do, but we don't get together often. And Lo, my oldest friend... Eugene is getting further and further away... as time goes on... and gas prices go higher. So I wonder if my "collective" consciousness is a bit under developed... or if I'm just ignorant of how much the collective affects me. Social consciousness is like a great beast that lumbers along, now and then shaking itself, like a dog out of water, and then lumbers on, looking for something to feed itself.

I'm sure you still suffer a great sense of loss with the death of your wife, Karen. How could you not? Her energy still lives inside of you. Or at least that energy within you that she connected to and brought alive and burning into your everyday life. Love does not bend with time, as William the playwright said, or something like that. Yes, the form may well change, but let us not confuse form with the energy that creates form and is ever changing these forms. I do not understand the other way—the way so many people seem to feel and live. How can you love someone and then later hate or despise that person? I can understand choosing not to have that person in your life anymore because, for whatever reason, that person's influence is no longer beneficial or acceptable to your life and consciousness.

I seem to be rambling now. So, I will end this attempt at writing an essay.

Oh, you've expressed in your own beautifully articulate words much of these thoughts in a letter early this spring and I was planning to comment on something you wrote but never found the right moment:

236

By way of preliminaries, I've never identified myself in the usual ways. The process of identification, of selecting patterns to call "I," "me," "myself," is subtle and usually hidden from our awareness. Most people identify with their body, or feelings, or thoughts, although we can also identify with patterns, roles, and archetypes. In our culture, the most usual self-identification is with our social or biological role: "I" am a man or a woman, a parent or a child, a certain occupation—doctor, lawyer, farmer, Indian chief. Or we take our sense of self from our family history, our genetics and heredity. Sometimes our sense of who we are is taken from our desires: sexual, aesthetic, or spiritual. For some, identity derives from our intellect, or our astrological sign. Some people choose an archetype, of hero, lover, mother, adventurer, clown, or thief, and live their whole life based on that.

For myself, I realized that I was not my body many, many years ago, in my 20s. I certainly never identified with my job. It took some decades to realize that I was not my mind, my intellect, either, but eventually I did. For the last twenty years I've dimly perceived that I am a spirit, but I've never been able to be precise about it. I agree with a line I've heard in AA, albeit rarely: we are not human beings having a spiritual experience, but spiritual beings having a human experience. But what does that mean? I've come to see my sense of self, a very human sense of self, as a play of patterns, and the world, too, as a play of patterns, but I cannot determine, either intellectually or intuitively, the shape of those patterns as clearly as I would like.

...In the end, things, people, and tasks die or change or we lose them. Nothing is exempt, including my body and mind. Spiritual practice, especially meditation, has taught me that I don't even possess my own experience. I do not invite my thoughts, nor do I own them. Many times have I wished some thoughts would stop, but they never do. There's been many times I wished certain thoughts would arise, but they do not come at my bidding. In fact, my thoughts seem to think

237

themselves, arising and passing according to their nature. The same is true of my feelings; I do not control them. My feelings often seem to me like the weather: rain and thunder one day, sunny skies the next, all changing according to certain conditions. One day I'm happy, the next day I'm sad, and at various times during a single day I can feel irritated, excited, restless, or contented, at peace. Where do these feelings, moods, and emotions come from? My body, too, follows its own laws....

I might add here that, yes, the body follows its own laws but (there are so many buts in life) the mental and emotional actions certainly help shape the direction or expression of those laws. And maybe they are only laws because somewhere, sometime, in the evolution of our human consciousness we accepted them as laws. But, then again, maybe we had no choice in how we viewed or experienced these "laws." We vibrate with a certain frequency that's particular to humans and humans alone, and that's why we see things the way we see things and why we're not a tree, a toad, or a rock. Anyway, that's a side thought. You have expressed your position quite clearly and, I will add, my position as clearly: *We do not know.*

So we read what others have thought and experienced and we go with what resonates with the core of our being. Or, as with most people, with the core of their social consciousness. Did the Ancients have a better view of the stars and of the origin of the universe and their own existence than we do, right now? They certainly had fewer distractions than us, I would think; but they also had less exposure to different experiences. (However, just as with the Biblical writers and Jewish thinkers, we know little of their private lives. I understand Rumi's Master was murdered—or lived in fear of being murdered—by a rival teacher. So I take all their teachings and examples with a grain of salt. Just as I do my own thoughts.) These ancients Masters and thinkers were busy formulating a direction that we could follow. But their ancient directions, their religions, their philosophies, end where my essence begins.

In a historical sense, I believe that *now* is the time for us to harvest the best of their knowledge. You've chosen the essential teachings of Buddhism, coupled with AA, to give formal shape and continuity to your way. You might consider these as training steps in the road of life. That doesn't mean, of course, you won't continue to practice and honor the principles you've learned in these teachings. (Just as I still carry the Deep Feeling Work I did in the 1980s.) You've come with these teachings to the edge of the known world. Now, you're on your own. In the sense that you have to trust your own play of patterns. I know, it doesn't seem so grand, does it? It feels like so much "not this, not that" because it is "not this, not that." We have to trust that place. We can just as easily say, "I AM THAT." But then everyone wants you to define THAT. And you have... already.

To be at ease with your own play of patterns... and know that your play of patterns holds as much truth as Ludwig Wittgenstein's play of patterns... as the tree's play of patterns... or the toad's play of patterns... but... and this is a tiny, big old stumbling but... if you want something greater, grander, than who you are... something that doesn't feel so "empty"... so "not this, not that"... I suppose you could think of yourself as both the space that holds the cup together (inside and out) and the particular moment in time that allows the space to hold this cup together... or is it the other way around? Anyway, you have to be both, as you've pointed out. It's a bit complicated for my head. As long as the cup will hold water....

And I'll drink to that.

Rummaging around in the basement
A confessional poem

...just as the sludge at the bottom of a lake is hidden
by clear, sparkling water.
—Irène Némirovsky
trans. Sandra Smith
All Our Worldly Goods
A Novel of Love Between the Wars

1 / Inner cave

There's a softness in me at times,
a weakness, like quicksand,
a human sink hole,
an overwhelming that panics me,
that threatens to cave in on me
and undermine everything I do,
and I must close my eyes tight
and fill this place—
this feeling that wants to throw in the towel,
that would welcome not being,
not being here in this world,
if only for a moment
this place that I can withstand only
by allowing God—
not some historical tyrant at war
with others of his kind,
not a religious idol, image, or concept,
some ancient king sitting on a golden throne;
but the creative, unknowable essence
of all that is—
to fill this vastness,

to remind me that I am spirit,
and have always been,
and that I exist because I am,
and for no other reason, or meaning,
or purpose, that you and I may understand.

2 / Enter self-doubt

Ambition does not inspire me.
Reputations do not awe me.
I place a golden halo over the head
of no man or woman,
nor do I worship unseen forces,
powerful they may be.
Fame may well escape me, indeed,
for I do not seek it.
(Yet, do not all poets want to be known and loved?)
Words do not come easily,
words of importance, that is.
The poet speaks with a voice
that belongs to all of us.
The poet—
man, woman or child—
contains his image, story,
and the image and story of each of us.
The poet burns a forever flame.
He flows, purifying his words as he goes.
He appears and disappears, elusive as the wind.
The poet breathes with the scent,
the rot, the colors, the hope and despair,
the aspirations of the earth;
he breathes with the heartbeat of the earth.
I am not this poet.
He has left me in the dust,

a pillar of self-doubt, ravaged
by my own self-inflicted arrows.

3 / Once more, with patience

I don't know how to say this,
this frustration I feel—
you know, to put the frustration into words
in a poem, to make them worthy,
so to speak.
Otherwise, it's just whining, more bitching.
"And the world bitches without pause,
there's no end to misery."
As a genuine poet, David Pendarus,
once said, a long time ago.

I inherited the genes from my mother,
this high-strung nervous system,
this unruly impatience.
Add to that, if you wish, that I'm a fire sign.
But so what?
"I alone am responsible for the evolution
of my soul."
Pendarus said that, a long time ago,
gazing out though the windows of his cell
in a Greek prison.
Right, now I know how Sisyphus must have felt.
Every day I stumble and fall,
pick myself up...and, like in the song,
start all over again...and again...and again.

4 / My own twisted drum beat

"Rage, rage, against the dying..."
& this rage, this anger,

—this continuous drum beat under my skin;
the plucking of an outrageous oud;
the sudden flaring of a flame;
an aborted gene of meanness—
springs out of me,
a monster hiding in the closet,
the boogeyman under the bed,
the body buried in the basement
suddenly come to life, a flash
searing through my brain and nerves,
tearing from my tongue,
ripping the air and the protective aura
of the other;
or lashing out at the ignorance
and stupidity of this world we've created,
like a stadium fan waving his arms,
yelling obscenities at the umpire,
screaming at the coach, the other players:
the enemy, myself, screaming
at God, tearing out my heart,
if only for a second, a moment,
then, just as quickly,
vanishing,
into remorse, at times,
into shame at others,
into psyche self-flagellation,
like those idiot monks who lash themselves
with whips on their backs,
for ecstasy, for forgiveness?
I don't know and I don't care
about their religious motivations.
It's my own twisted drum beat
in this journey toward the light
and release,

and absorption,
back into this beloved earth,
that captures my imagination,
this journey that has allowed me
to see my own terrors,
my own beauty.

5 / And in the darkest corner

Imagine a huge spider,
(or a rat or a poisonous snake).
Fear hides in the darkest corner
of this basement,
behind every pillar and stud and beam,
behind every moving box, every stack
of old books,
every nook and cranny;
for my anger, frustration, impatience,
all serve their petty tyrant
like branches on a fat tree,
but the tree itself, fear,
sends its roots deep into the limbs,
the twigs, the nerves, into the body;
and fear attempts to invade my soul,
guardian and protector of any action
that does not bear fruit from the heart:
the center of my being and the consciousness
that connects me to your center
and to the center of this that we call upon
without knowing its true name,
that some would liken to a mother's love
for her child,
for nothing shall stand between the two,
or threaten the child

for the child is none other than life;
and where does this life begin
if not before the beginning,
before earth and shape and form,
before the sun and spiraling galaxies,
before the point, the moment,
the no-time and no-space
in time and space where the mind
can no longer venture,
where you and I no longer go home
and there is no where or when or how
but only is.

6 / Not knowing

I don't know what purpose I write
these lines—no longer do I know
if for you or for me.
I feel like that song bird in the trees
outside my Portland window—
the one that's now singing:
but to whom? and for what purpose?

Do most poets feel this way?
(Or should I call myself a poet?)
Once I knew—or thought I knew.
My words, like arrows with bittersweet
barbs, I aimed for the closet heart,
the sleeping mind, the social zombie;
and, yes, I aimed those arrows,
much of the time,
at some beautiful woman,
her eyes wide shut, asleep in her life,
not seeing me or anyone real
in those lovely eyes.

How arrogant, my actions!
(But with the best of intentions,
no doubt.)
Just as in the evolution of dogness,
their sensitive noses dismissed, somehow,
the stench of their own shit,
as now they track it unwittingly into the house
and onto their pillow beds.

I walked on stilts,
in a manner of speaking,
the way poets often will.
But that's all gone: the chase,
the quest to awaken, the need to shake
the leaves in spring.

It's autumn now, a different season,
no time for lust or beauty stripped bare
like camel toes in your astonished face.
I honor that singing bird in my mind,
that sweet bird;
that wild flight of imagination,
and I go—I fly—with that backyard bird
to wherever the singing goes,
for that bird carries my heart in its song.

Winter, thinking of spring

"There has not been for a long time a spring
as beautiful as this one..."
wrote Czeslaw Milosz in 1936,
five years before I was born;
and now, this moment,
I'm looking out the kitchen window
of my Portland home—a home
across the street from a cemetery.

I'm staring at a layer of ice
and falling snow and cold eastern wind
layering the ground, the trees,
and the streets in white,
as our great nation seems to be coming undone,
ripping apart at the financial seams,
after years of an unpopular war and political
chicanery, lying and deceit.

But this thought now—
our departing President,
the falling snow, the cold (the harshest
in the Valley in nearly four decades),
these thoughts must be too transient for caring
in another one hundred years,
or ten thousand years,
by someone reading this poem,
(if someone should read this poem,
by luck or accident or merit).
Yet the seasons, coming and going,
the spinning of the earth,
the snow falling and the wind blowing,
the roses in my garden bent and broken with ice,

these things, these earthly things,
they go on and on.

Of this beautiful life-forming earth,
I see no end in sight,
until,
if we're still here,
the sun—our heavenly star—
explodes into supernova and blows us
and all that remains—our great cities,
our grand philosophies, our boiling kettle
of religions, our drug wars, our racial differences,
our porno sites, our man-made monuments
and the natural wonders of this world
—blows all these things to kingdom come.

But that is not my concern,
not my concern at all.

This coming new year:
year 2009 C.E,
the Oregon rains will come again,
the earth will spring forth life.
How beautiful this spring will be!

As I look out my kitchen window

Image a little girl bundled in winter clothes,
dancing on a small, green hillside,
dancing in a graveyard—
a hillside of plots called "Baby Land"—
this little girl dancing on a cold January day,
waving her arms in excitement to her younger sister,
who's just down the hillside, racing towards her.

As I look out my kitchen window,
across the street from this cemetery,
I see these scenes and ponder our beginnings
and our endings in time.
Luckily, these two girls have bypassed "Baby Land"
but neither they nor I nor you
shall avoid those other grownup passages,
those on the other hillsides—
below the ground or up in smoke.
That is, as far as these bodies go.

And how far do these bodies go?
How far did they come?
And shall they rise again someday?
I think not.
For, as we were here before time,
before these bodies, so shall we be again.

We exist now and shall always be.

No, not in a void of nothingness have we emerged,
embodying this shroud of dust like a treasure,
like our closest friend or a spouse or a lover,
this evolutionary body with its head and face,

249

its arms and legs, its organs and hormones.
I believe, without proof or psychic knowledge,
we, you and I, have hurled ourselves into time,
through a dynamics of consciousness
into this ever-changing, ever-passing world
before our senses,
emerging through earth, in ice and wind and fire,
in blood and bone,
nurtured by the soul and the human heart,
that which we truly are but that which neither you nor I
nor those little girls dancing over graves
can rightly name.

The Dusty Traveler
I sing this moment

I'm sitting on a tall, wooden stool
in the island of our kitchen—
the cemetery across the street
on view through the window box
above the kitchen sink—
and I begin, for the first time,
to read a book of poems by the Polish poet
Adam Zagajewski, a book called
Mysticism for Beginners.

How clear and beautiful his language!

So this is mysticism, more than magical,
the human dark streaked with burnt and burning
stars, crowded streets made of terrifying shadows,
dreams, light; as breathtaking as the sight
of that young deer appearing out of nowhere
in the cemetery across the street on a cold morning
many moons ago.

I am no mystic, no prophet,
but simply a man sitting at his kitchen window
on this January day, a few days
after the inauguration of my country's
first African-American president,
following more than two hundred years
of domination of one color over another,
        of slavery, lynchings—
"There is no lavender word for lynch,"
wrote Langston Hughes—
segregation, discrimination, Jim Crow laws.

I grew up in the South and witnessed
without understanding, I was just a kid,
those white devils in whiter sheets
with blind holes for eyes that could not see
as they drove by on Hwy 78
in their terrorist procession of fear and hate.

Now, this day, this week, like Whitman before me,
like Langston Hughes, I, too, sing America.

I sing these United States, the possibility, the promise,
for America has always been a dusty traveler on the road,
a spark of consciousness, twisted
hither and thither in the winds of ambition,
arrogance, greed, pride, and fear;
but a spark, nevertheless,
that must light up our human hearts,
if ever we are to journey onward to being free
in this political, this passing world.

Or else, perhaps, we shall all perish.

I sing this moment, this bridge, this opening,
between colors, between our earthly home
and the distant stars,
between people, animals, trees, rocks;
between you and me, whoever you are,
as we travel together through darkness
and the shadows that would scare us to death
in this world on this jewel of a planet earth.

January 2009

Once upon a time,
A love story
of timeless and personal proportions
Or,
in the words of Emily Dickinson,
"a route of evanescence"

Traveler, you must set forth
At dawn
I promise marvels of the holy hour…
    —Wole Soyinka, *The Road*

I come from everywhere,
To everywhere I'm bound….
        —José Martí, *Simple Verses*

It was a long road here—a difficult road.
The road is yours now. You hold it
the way you hold your friend's hand and count his pulse
on this scar left by the handcuffs.
A normal pulse. A sure hand. A sure road.
    —Yannis Ritsos, "The Blackened Pot"

This is not the first time...
and may not be the last.
    —David Pendarus

The road, any road, away from childhood,
kudzu forts, Baptist churches, rock fights,
BB battles in the oak and pine tree woods,
honeysuckles and wild plums in the hollow,
chiggers in the blackberries, itching like crazy,
homemade scuppernong wine, swinging

like Tarzan across the creek
on muscadine vines,
(eyes wide open for cottonmouths),
and those damn red old hills of Georgia.

A beautiful girl, my age, 17 years,
orange blossoms in the scent of her young body,
she enters my heart like a sharp knife.
I hitchhike 500 miles to see her,
Atlanta to Tampa;
turn around,
and hitchhike back the next day.
In our innocence, we mistake this distance
for the 12th of Never.

Books: an escape, a promise, a passion.
Like Jack Kerouac, I crisscross these states,
my thumb out ,
all the way to the Great Northwest
and the Seattle World's Fair.
I do not have a beatific vision,
I see only a strange and wondrous land
and a few good people, and some not so much.

Along comes the Bay of Pigs.
I'm in college in central Florida and we're all holding
our breath and waiting...waiting.

President Kennedy is murdered in Dallas;
Martin Luther King in Memphis.
Marilyn Monroe...there are questions.

A Jewish girl in love with T. S. Eliot
and F. Scott Fitzgerald,
a Jewish girl from New York City,

playing hide-and-seek,
brown hair in a Southern wind,
brown hair blowing over her mouth,
confused and torn and bewitching.
My best college bud.
We will always be friends.

Oh, look!
In the middle of the garden, a stone,
a stone in the middle of the garden!

*****

My best friend from high school dies in a hospital;
at the same time, in another hospital, in Atlanta,
his wife, gives birth to their first child.
The following spring, 1966,
my oldest brother kills himself in a parked car,
leaving a wife and 5 kids.
Meanwhile...back in the jungle...
My other brother, Jack the storyteller,
two-tour USMC hero, and a natural warrior
fights an unseen enemy in the napalmed trees
of Viet Nam and Cambodia.
Meanwhile...back in the States...
I'm on the other side, a natural peacemaker,
marching for peace in Eugene, Oregon.

A dead bird covered with ants...
a lover's nest in any tree, sounds good
to me, as long as your spirit comes along.
Drugs, sure, if they'll help us see,
get me through the darkness,
make me laugh,
and show me who you are, really.

A piano player, blonde keys in the wind
on the intersection of High Street
and University Avenue...
another man's wife...stolen moments...
listening for her footsteps coming up the stairs...
blonde legs under and over mind.
Oh, god, you are so beautiful.
A spiritual revelation in her arms.
A kiss vanishing on the lips.
Even God must be lonely at night.

An artist, a painter, her face morphing
into an illumination; *"she comes
in colors
everywhere"*;
street riots and psychedelic
hang men in the flowers of San Francisco.

Come and see the smoke in the streets.
Come and see
the smoke in the streets.
Come and see the smoke in the streets!

Doug Blazek's old tabletop letterpress,
a handful of words, printed and bound...
myself: *inside out.*
As Lew Welch says in "Words to That Effect":
                    "how
can you write a
poem except from the
inside out?"
Letters ripped from a Bellevue bed.
Convolution hides from the truth.
On my wallpaper the flowers are dying.

Always on the sunny side, like Henry Miller.
But a dead angel my watermark.

*****

Thirty years...
stop and go...stop and go.
Like a traffic jam on the freeway.

You say I repeat myself;
very well, I repeat myself.
A man on fire, my heart run amuck.

Saturn returns—
Something has to change!
Who am I?
How can I even answer that question!
Listening to Dylan...thousands of pages
into Carl Jung...my cup overfloweth...
Dancing to "Zorba"...Janis Jopin
and Country Joe live at the Fillmore...
Pondering Jane Roberts' *The Nature of Personal Reality.*
Rumi...Issa...Basho...Kabir...the Chinese poets.
Lorca...Neruda...the French symbolists.
Carlos Castaneda...Krishnamurti.
Ramana Maharshi...Suzki...R. H. Blyth.
Yearning for enlightenment... for the Source.
(The source of all that is.)

We humans love to tell stories.
We love tall tales:
Witness the Greek myths, the Holy Bible, Krishna,
John Henry and Billie the Kid.
Stories mask the great mystery
of who we are and why we do things.

And the poets?
What about the poets you say!
Where are the poems that will open people's hearts?
(I don't give a damn about your manifestos;
your theories of pure poetry.
Or your swans and peacocks, your Muse,
your ancient dragons,
or the worn-out gods you worship.)
The poets—the respectable ones—
the ones who win the rewards
and get books published by respectable publishers—
they hold diplomatic positions or teach
at universities, "to make a living."
A few get christened Poet Laureate of this state,
or that state, or even the nation.
The others: the "underground poets,"
"the living poets," "the outlaw poets,"
mostly they wash your windows,
mow your lawns, deliver your mail; and some go mad,
or, like d.a. levy, they shoot themselves in Cleveland.
Bukowski lives in turmoil, an old man dying in a room.
In L.A., for God's sake!
Snyder takes refuge in a Zen monastery.
T. L. Kryss draws rabbits and moves through
his poems
as quietly as a ghost.
Blazek is everywhere,
but can't seem to get anywhere;
and even I have difficulty understanding his poems,
the way he twists and wrings the language into meaning.
Willie, he's dervish dancing somewhere in India.
Joel Deutsch, Brown Miller, D. R. Wagner,
God knows what they're doing.

In Russia, and a dozen other legal states,
these poets would be shot or thrown in prison.
As for myself,
if I were a poet,
I'd be one of them, thank you.
(At least, I'd aspire to be.)
But that's just the way I am.
On second thought,
can you even be an outlaw poet in the USA?
Perhaps I should have been a ventriloquist.
Or an organic farmer?

Night falls in the rain.
And it rains...and rains.
40 days and nights, perhaps.
I'm not sure.
I have difficulty with time.
For, like you, I'm older than time itself.
Older than the universe.
Not me personally, you understand.
But who I am, beneath this,
beneath all this that you see,
beneath all my talking.
(Or within, if you prefer.)

The rains fall,
fall without ceasing in the Valley.
I get brain rot; I grow web feet.
Perhaps I even quack like a duck!
The basement's flooded with old crimes.
I'm checking the roof.
I'm looking under the bed.
I'm swearing at the doors and windows,
all stuck tight as the rain continues.

I'm fractured by self-doubts, anger, despair.
Visions arrive in fits and starts and handjobs.
Desires flood mind and body.
Ideas float upon my imagination like seahorses
upon the high seas.

The rain falls, morning and night,
falls without ceasing in the Valley.
I sing in tune with J. J. Cale:
"Ain't no change in the rain, ain't no change in this pain."

There's an old joke about Portland rain.
A woman visiting our fair city for the first time,
umbrella in hand, stops a boy riding his bike
on the sidewalk, and she asks the boy,
"Boy, does it ever stop raining in Portland?"
And the boy answers, "How should I know?
I'm only 6!"

As a boy, I loved the sound of rain
falling on the tin roof of our old farm house,
my brother telling me stories—
but this...this...
wet mornings, wet evening, wet dreams,
everything dissolving in time and water.
Drowning, I think, must be a long way to walk.

Hope.
Hope: the last refuge of an evolving humanity,
stretches ever more before us,
before each of us,
to embrace our unshakable faith
that everything will work out for the best.

Hope.
Hope is...
I don't like definitions—
definitions impose limitations,
here a wall, there a wall—
but here goes,
I'll work within these limitations.
As Carlos Drummond said,
or perhaps Blaze Cendars?
"hemmed in lives grow densest."

Hope is...
that the next bottle of wine you buy
under ten dollars
will surprise and delight you.
(Most of the time,
William Blake couldn't even afford wine.)

Hope is...
that we can stay up after midnight,
and let it all hang out,
and not fall down on our faces.

Hope is...
that the girl you fell in love with on the city bus—
you never said a word,
only a glance between you—
will get off at the same stop you get off.

Hope is...
that the ripening strawberries in your patch
won't rot on the vine
or be devoured by slimy slugs;
that the garden irises in your garden,
their heavy blooms bent to the earth,

will somehow...someway...survive this rain,
this rain that keeps falling day and night,
this rain that keeps falling in my dreams
and in my thoughts.

Hope is...
that the philosopher Hume—
Remember him from your university days?—
will look you straight in the eye,
from the grave,
and assure you that the rain, this rain,
will stop...eventually,
and the sun will shine tomorrow.
(For sure! Wait and see!)
Until then: hold on...carry on.

Hope is that that the next poem you write—
if you write poems—
will, finally,
at last,
hallelujah!
capture the essence of Truth and Beauty.
Or, at least, cast a spell on that pretty girl
you saw on the city bus,
a spell that will open her eyes
to the wonders of who she is .

Hope is...
that, by traveling light,
you will catch up with the light within you,
the light you see in your dreams,
the forever light within each of us.

Hope is...
that you're not chasing your own tail,

that the wheels you're spinning belong to the Sun's chariot,
as you race through darkness and into your destiny.
(If you believe in destiny.)

Hope is faith in the Unknown.

*****

What can you do?
As another prisoner in a Greek jail,
a man falsely imprisoned,
would later, in a moment of resignation,
say to his fellow prisoners.

What can you do?
I throw in the towel. I give up.
I surrender to the Unknown.
I let go.
Come what may!

And then, with no effort on my part,
just like that,
here comes the sun.

*****

A wedding in the Washington woods,
a marriage in a sunny meadow,
a marriage "Made in Heaven"—an August event.
Dark clouds, and my own self doubts,
vanish in obedience to the sun and a gentle wind,
breathtaking as a shooting star,
from the Unknown.
Honeymooning, the two of us,
backpacking in a foreign land.
Ah, those were the days,
we thought they'd go on and on;

not counting on hostile laws, religion,
and a Greek prison.

What was I thinking?

Lamentations upon lamentations!
Two years in prison for growing hashish,
"the black smoke."
What, those ten scrawny weeds?

I evoke the words of Walt Whitman:
"All has been gentle with me, I keep no account with
lamentations,
(What have I to do with lamentations?)"

I begin my novel on the fly, so to speak.
Thirty years later I'm still writing,
Enough! Or too much!

I am not a brave man. Defiant, yes;
I question authority, including my own,
as I question the validity of any premise
not borne out by experience or reason,
especially if it comes from fear,
especially if it has no room for laughter
that vibrates from heart and belly,
and surely your perceptions of the world
differ from mine, and that's your truth,
and I honor the God within you.

The restless years, you called them,
as I watched you spellbound in the Grecian light.
I could not take my eyes from your beauty,
your spirit an endless curving road,
free and lovely as spring in an ever-changing

264

field of wildflowers,
like woodland fairies dancing on the banks
of Sunflower River.

Home again...
land of tall evergreens, Oregon rain...
going our separate ways...
(Thomas Wolfe, you were right.
Home, like Odysseus' horizon,
shimmers ever beyond our reach).
A cold wind on the beach at night biting my ears,
as I listen and witness the origin of the universe
roaring into manifestation with stars, planets,
this earth that I love.
A vision? A dream? An hallucination?
I am glad, I am so glad for the warm fire at my back
and friends with a bottle of wine.

*****

The tide always comes back in.
My heart run amuck… again.
Husband and wife, home and hearth,
a child to raise,
steady work at a day job,
counting the hours, the minutes, till I'm in your arms
and we're knocking on heaven's door,
two awakening souls, looking for what?
Liberation? Wholeness?
If only we knew how to heal the pain inside.
Oh, god, you are so beautiful, dancing,
dancing naked in the mirror.

*****

"Love without freedom
is like a fire without air.
A fire without air goes out."
—Mma Ramotswe
The Double Comfort Safari Club,
Alexander McCall Smith

But we're both afraid...
afraid of losing each other.
And that's exactly what happens.

Does the fear itself manifest what we dread?
Or do we know, somewhere deep within,
that what we most fear is, indeed,
a portion of our destiny?

Do what scares you the most.
A wise man once said to me.

There's no way out.
No way to sidestep the fear.
No way to deny.
We must experience the origin of the fear.
We must acknowledge this fear.
To reach the other side,
we must go through this fear.

*****

An ideal, twisted and broken as a tree limb
in an ice storm, this marriage,
ash spewing in the air,
Mt. St Helens raining down on our lives...
humiliation, separation, betrayal...
this 1910 house for sale...
drinking and dancing, running on fear and despair

and a knowledge that somewhere, somehow, someday,
this will all make sense...or else it won't.

*****

A woman, light as a hawk's feather, subtle
as flower essence, powerful as the reach
of ancient myths, symbols, and civilizations,
taking my hand in a never-ending spiral,
guiding me to a Teacher, psyche eyes
through loving waves penetrating my soul,
shattering my defenses, cracking my shell—
my brilliant coat of false colors—pushing
me to the very edge of existence,
my rage spewing out at all that we call holy:
Mother, God, this body—
my hands wanting to rip out this heart of mine;
then stillness, silence...
the circle spiraling inward on itself.

A 30,000 year old warrior breathing new life
into this forever road, allowing me, forgiving
me my errors, my indulgences, blasting me
with runners of such truth and beauty
I could only weep as if these tears
would never end.

Years of solitude...a meditation on the Source
(the Source of all that I am and all that is).
A reckoning, a lesson, nothing is lost,
a doctor's touch, a kiss vanishing on the lips,
all is grist for the mill: rain that pours down,
that soaks the ground and floods the land,
a river that returns to its source and begins the trip
homeward, all over again.

*****

Endless all that I am
and endless this journey to you...

A companion, true and steady as my own soul,
now settled in place, a home overlooking the city,
a city that witnessed so much pain in each of us.
You are beautiful, my dear, so contrary, a healing tonic
to my defeated romanticism and ravaging self-doubts,
my folly, frenzy, and ignorance.
"Kind and respectable," as one of her Spanish pupils,
a second-grade boy, a troubled-student,
writes in a valentine to her.

A story book about time and love and destiny,
this passing world....
This time in my own voice,
with a little help from my friends.

Grandkids playing and squabbling in the living room.
My own private garden...a simple life.
As cars and cycles swish by on the road,
the road between our house and the cemetery...
the road in a nut shell.

We're not here, then we're here,
then we're not...again.

And all that remains will be what we give each other.

It's Your Birthday: November 30, 2009........ for Don

It's your birthday raise the flag make the sun come
out raise those puny little plants covered in mud and
soaked in sky flooded vapors

It's your birthday are you sitting in silence drinking
some latte laced liquid wishing for a pastry cream
oozing out the side of your mouth imagining a young
sweet thing lavishing her soft skin her subtle form
along your long leg curling slinking slowly her eyes
falling swiftly to meet your own as a glance involves
only a hint a tender second of longing for the body
remembered from time past

It's your birthday raise those roof beams you
carpenters you rug layers or was that layers of bugs
from years past when cockroaches were the craze in
the haze and Florida sun swept the rain-soaked winds
to collide lazily and crazily with palm trees swaying
and praying and old Anne Pfeiffer never had it so
good in that Chapel as socialized protestants gazed
into the eyes of one very large Dr. Eckleberg peering
down through glasses on high trying to avoid the
lines of mind imprisonment

It's your birthday did you know it then when reading
and underlining and following a French student's
breasts around the old campus pavements finding
translations a bit too existential and delirious even
then for the sixties

And so it's your birthday old man not really such an
old man but yes an old friend that I love and cherish
the words uttered and muttered for so many years
and days and hours upon this daylit computer toy

Indeed it is your day of birth today some sixty-eight
years ago in the back roads of Georgia where spiritual
substance and lazy day sunshine were your strength
your survival your way to grab that light that would
shed the slight fragrance of life along your path

Indeed it was an Autumn day that brought you to this
world of form and woods and books with stories and
fantasy forms to help you walk along the stretch
ahead holding out your hand through storms of
words and pages and hours that let time pass to this
day yet another in the gentle cloth of truth

Always in my heart
Always

11.30.2009

Birthday poem by Lo Caudle

Returning to the future

We are the Ancient Ones,
you and I.
We speak the Old Language.
These words; just this.

Look around you.

The New Language has little meaning
to us, to you and I,
for we have stumbled—or discovered?
or returned?—into the deep silence:
that sound beneath all spoken words.

Our voices, long ago singing, singing,
all, all, breaking ground that's now
turned into a graveyard—monuments,
sea stones, rounded and smoothed,
till our voices only whisper to us,
telling us what we knew and loved and lost,
what we've forgotten, left behind,
what no longer concerns us.
For we belong to the Ancients,
you and I,
our voices muffled by waves,
torn by wind and tossed in the fire.

We speak no more in tongues
like the wonderful and terrifying machines
they've invented to enslave and free us,
like all machines eventually do.

We, the Ancient Ones, wrap ourselves
in ultimate silence, like grass seed
in the darkness of rich soil,
and we shall come again, bearing gifts.
We shall appear as voices in your dreams,
in your secret thoughts, your desires,
in the space between heart beats,
in the quietness, in the silence,
in the night.

What will you take with you?

What will you take with you
as you leave this earth,
this glorious blue planet swirling in space?
What will you take with you
when you go?

The hands on my desk clock
point to six in the evening.
Will you take time?
Will you take the memory of this moment,
the memory of every moment,
with you?

Lily Poo, still a puppy,
shows no interest in poetry or metaphysics,
as she gnaws on a bone on my favorite rug
and looks to me for directions,
whirling her piebald tail like a helicopter.
Will you take the love I feel
for this impish dachshund with you?
The love I feel for my friends and family?

Will you take the nocturnes
of Chopin? The wind in spring
leafing trees outside my window?
The lovely days of May,
the dancing butterflies in my Mother's garden;
the scent of pine trees;
October's return
and November transformations?

Will you take my anticipation
as I wait for the woman I love to return home,
after teaching immigrant children all day
to speak and write a new language?

Will you take this glass of red wine,
the taste in my mouth,
the grape, the earth, the sun, the soil, the rain?
Will you take this,
all that I see and feel and think
and all that I hold close to my heart?
Will you take me with you?

June 2010

Some people think

Some people
think that
hobbling around on
frail legs
with a
smile on
your face
is dying
with dignity.
—John Bennett
"Dying with Dignity"

And some people
think,
I suppose
they think,
the world is flat,
like stale beer.
And some people
think,
I suppose
they think,
The moon is made
of green cheese,
moldy...
to boot.
And some people
think,
I suppose
they think,
Crazy John Bennett
is crazy
as 100 mph
on a hair-pin curve
just under a blonde's
left eye.

On the mother of all roads

Each man's life represents a road toward himself,
an attempt at such a road, the intimation of a path.
—Hermann Hesse, *Demian*

We travel a pathway of stone,
a road that appears to be light,
a road that soon turns into a flowing river,
a river that leads us onward into a dark woods,
and, then, before our enchanted eyes,
the river vanishes altogether
into deep shadows,
self-doubts,
and etheric mists,
dreams that terrify us,
dreams that carry intimations of a truth
behind the Light—
behind the metaphor and the symbol,
behind the teachings and the mythology,
behind the experiences and the vision,
behind all these illusions,
a truth that points like a Zen koan
to the source of all that is,
and I am one with this source,
and I am becoming one with this source,
as surely as the gods, our brothers and sisters,
as surely as you are.

Falling in love

Ah, youth and old age,
I fell in love, never-ending love,
more times than I could count!
"Only you...and you alone..."
Only is just a four letter word.
(Besides, who's counting?)

At first, we believe it's the Other we love.
Then we discover the Other lives inside of us,
and it's a great mystery, a great mystery indeed,
how specific the ones we love show up,
just in time,
to take us from certainty into not-knowing,
from death into life.

It's a great mistake, but a mistake we make,
to assume you are who you think you are.

Let us now praise famous poets

But what are the poets to us?
All seven million!
What is history, yours and mine,
and all that's gone and left its mark
upon this earth,
when everything changes,
when everything comes to an end,
even time;
when you and I are no longer
you and I?

So many intersections on the road,
so many choices.
Or so it appears.
But do we really have a choice
other than to choose who we are
becoming?
And who we are becoming,
is that not the Great Unknown?

Why should it matter then to us—
to you and me,
who are bounded by time and space?
(If we are bounded by time and space.)
Why does it matter if we maintain order,
rather than give in to chaos,
when we do not even know what we are,
or what this is all around us:
the cosmos, a tree, a beloved pet
that will follow you out the door
no matter where you're going?

But it does matter, doesn't' it?

So don't even think that you know who I am,
or what a poem is,
or a tree, or the cosmos.

Don't even think that I know
what is
and what is not true.
Or who I am becoming.

And that's why this tale is a jest,
a koan,
a fast ball with a curve.

Here I am. Or am I not?

Late thoughts
Where did the morning go?

2011-2012

Look closely, old poet, look closely into your hands
for in your hands you will see
the lights of home.
Look deeply, old poet, into the eyes of those you love
and into the heart of all that is.

§

All so vague:
In autumn the reasons why
All fall
away
And there's just this
Inexplicable sadness.
—Saigyō , *Mirror For the Moon*, 12th c.
trans. William R. LaFleur

§

He had no address;
he lived in a ball of dust
playing with the universe.
Ancient Sanskrit Manuscript / Essential Zen

In between, I am becoming

"Both...and..."

In between spirit and matter,
I am becoming.

In between good and evil,
between this and that,
I am becoming.

In between left and right,
above and below,
darkness and light,
I am becoming.

In between day and night,
pleasure and pain,
heaven and earth,
time and space,
I am becoming.

In between fire and water,
earth and air,
instinct and civilization,
feeling and intellect,
kindness and cruelty,
I am becoming

In between war and peace,
male and female,
duality and oneness,
law and mercy,
synthesis and analysis,
divine and human,
I am becoming.

I could go on.
Or not.

In between fear and love,
desire and thought,
I am becoming.

In between ignorance and knowledge,
I am becoming.
(All ignorance is ignorance of self;
all knowledge is knowledge of self.)

In between the crack of the worlds,
I am becoming.

I am becoming who I am.

I am becoming to you.

We're here or we're not

We exist in a black and white world,
in essence—
we're here or we're not here.
Each moment, we make a single choice:
Yes? No?
We breathe in; we breathe out.
But even the human heart sometimes
skips a beat.
We live, these everyday lives,
these lives of love
and lives of fear denying love,
on the edge of light,
in a world of shadows,
a world of grays,
a world of differences, slight and major;
a world of measurements and degrees,
like the weather, like greatness.

We're here or we're not here.
A door opens; a door closes.
The same door: you.

10,000 years from now

Think,
(if you will),
1,000 years from now,
or, if you prefer,
10,000 years from this time,
from the moment you no longer
live on this earth,
you no longer exist in a body,
where will you be,
10,000 years from now?

Where are your ambitions,
your aspirations,
your prized recognitions,
your personal accomplishments:
all those things you loved and prized,
where are they,
10,000 years from now?

Once you're dead,
you're dead forever.

Unless, of course, you're not.

If you're not,
if you're not dead,
if you've only left a body,
a personality, a life, a memory,
a relationship, a secret,
behind you,
where are you?

What do you believe?
Say you believe
in the Christian scriptures;
or the Muslim;
or the Buddhist—
if belief determines your fate,
does that not mean, not
the particulates of your belief,
but the very belief itself,
does this determine your afterlife?

(If there is an afterlife
or no afterlife—
does that depend on
what you believe?)

If you don't believe in an afterlife,
does your life just disappear?
You just vanish, all that you are
and all that you might have become?

Tell me, which belief gives you
what you truly want?
(Since we face the Unknown,
not knowing
what is and what isn't?
Or is that simply my belief?
Do we really know, for sure,
what lies beyond?)

Oh, come on,
don't monkey mind me,

or chatter me up
with what you've read
(in all the books you've read),
or twitter what you've heard,
or what you've been told;
but tell me,
from all your experiences,
what do you know?

What belief gives you freedom?
Or unlimitedness?
Or hope?
What belief makes you despair?
(Hope springs eternally from the roots
of despair and desire.)
What belief gives you what you most desire?

Why are we here?

Why are we here?
On this earth, this planet?
We come up with so many reasons,
do we not?
We're just here,
no questions asked.
Just seek pleasure and avoid pain.
A fair enough but limited philosophy.

We're here to learn lessons.
Many spiritual people believe this.

We're here to worship the gods;
to service the king's pleasure;
or to deny ourselves and live for what comes after.

Believe me, like the Ancient Greek thinkers,
I'm at a loss to explain what all this is,
this that is;
where we come from, why we're here,
and where we're going.

We can always make up a likely story,
just as we've done for thousands of years.

Ramtha, a master teacher,
once said to a group of seekers,
myself included:
"You're here because you want to be here!"

Desire...this great outreaching
for something—
this continuous seeking to gather knowledge
or experiences or power,
fame or immortality, profit or prophesies,
everything you can name under the sun,
and this thing, this elusive thing
that cannot be named—
how this life force has been religiously discouraged,
even downright condemned, throughout the ages!

To desire not to desire—
Is this the path to liberation?
From what? From desire?
From sticky emotions?
From suffering?
From the angst of who and what we are?

This world we live in

How the earth came to be,
do we know?
God? The Big Bang?
(If there's no one to hear,
can there really be a bang?
If no mirrors exist, can God exist?)

Perhaps the world came to be,
as Einstein may well have believed,
through a creative moving force
far beyond our historical concepts of God
and time and space?

It is what it is becoming,
what more can we honestly say?

But the world, this grand contraption,
the world we live in, *this*
we have created,
together,
this and all the many worlds we may live in:
all things beautiful and grotesque,
all things sinful and terrifying,
all things we measure with our human mind.

This world we live in,
this
we create moment by moment.
Out of what?
Out of the raw possibilities of spirit?
Out of the great unknown?
Out of you, whoever you are?

As if you had never been alive

To our Great Unknown Mother-Father,
who lives inside each of us

To be born and to die,
and never to be recognized
for who and what you are,
as if you had never been alive!

To travel through time and space,
to arrive by bus, by train, by boat
or ship, or spaceship even,
to arrive in a place
and never to be seen and known
for who you are,
as if you had never been alive!

A friend passes away, a close friend;
a hundred years comes and goes,
as do you,
both of you forgotten,
as if you had never been alive!

To just *disappear*...
In countries all over the world, every day
this goes on,
as if you had never been alive!

In time,
4.5 billion years from now,
our Sun will explode in a mighty
nuclear orgasm,
vaporizing this blue gem Earth.

If that doesn't wipe us out,
they say, in time,
another billion years or so,
our Milky Way Galaxy will collide
with the Andromeda Galaxy.
But you and I, we will be long gone
before then,
as if we had never been born!

To be here on this Earth,
to come face to face
with the mystifying Unknown,
and to not awaken, my friend,
to who you are,
as if you had never been alive,
do not allow this to happen!

O Great Mother-Father:
the life-forming Love that lives
within each of us:
the Light within all stars:
the Dark Energy in all matter:
the Intelligence in all structures:
the Will in my individual will:
the Consciousness in each moment:
the Gravity that holds us in place,
or destroys us:
I pray,
do not let this happen to your children,
do not let us disappear,
as if we had never been alive!

As long as the fires keep burning

Is it gold? Is it brass?
So hard to tell in this light!
—David Pendarus
"In the shadow land of famous poets"

Let me count the poets.
No, no, their numbers, like the stars,
overpower my ability to calculate!
A swarm of egos, these wasters of words,
posturing and buzzing in the night,
pestering both time and history,
stealing everything in sight
(like the poets before them).
Like children, they are:
"Look at me, look at me!"

Timid souls, these poets,
who protect the sand they're playing on.
Some, like good bureaucrats or factory workers,
these poets go into work each day, every day,
to write their immortal poems,
the way literary professors, writing classes,
and other poets have told them how it's done.

Still others, not so timid or obedient,
(you know who you are),
turn over earth and spirit to form rock
and marbled monuments,
some even plowing fresh ground.

Others, gasping for hidden truths,
like fish riding a bicycle for the first time,
venture into subterranean passages,
long buried by the veneer
of religion, politics and social graves.

A few, fascinated by the light,
leap into the darkness—
a darkness,
where,
only a moment ago,
there burned a bright flame.

We praise those fragmented souls,
longing for wholeness,
who walk with eyes wide shut into the fire,
a fire that consumes all that is false within them.

As long as the fires keep burning,
as long as we keep the human spirit alive
on this Earth,
does it matter who?
Does it matter who keeps the fire burning?

Gravity always wins,
and a dog,
they say,
is never wrong
Or,
Watch out for that falling apple!

1

Cheers for the Three Graces:
hydrogen, gravity, and time.
Dark matter holds everything together,
the scientists tell us.
Or is it the gray matter of *not knowing?*

2

The dragons of doubt must be resolved,
abandoned and vanquished,
not by warring with yourself
but by picking up the other end of the stick,
by letting go attractions to your hidden doubts
and allowing what you truly want—
not in some distant future
but in this moment, here, now.

3

Once upon a time I looked so young.
Now I look so old.
Have you noticed that we don't see space?
We can only see objects in space:
a stone in the middle of the road,
a falling leaf, a closed door, a star in the night sky,
a seahorse in sea grass,
a kitchen wall, the sun and moon, a face,
a disaster on the road.

And time?

Love, has no sides,
no directions, no polarity.
Let your existence speak for love.

4

Spiritual vampires, you might call them.
They go to church, to the mosque, to the temple.
They practice meditation,
they feed on the blood—
the life force—
of Jesus, of Mohammed, of Buddha.
What do you feed on?

5

Put a man and a woman together and soon,
all too soon,
like an electrical cord in the garage,
or Christmas lights from the year before,
they're tangled up in knots.

Love has no object, no Other.
Yet, in this, our human embodiment,
we desire the other.
We seek out another,
be it man or woman,
god or goddess,
a creature, a plant, a rock,
a substance,
a form, an idea, an image—
to express, to know, to experience,
love's universal nature,
in this that we are the particular.

6

How strange, all this.
I don't know how much I like not knowing,
not knowing what this is, *this that is,*
but only how we define this or that.

How strange,
to see people who know
for certain the mind of God —
what God wants of us.
(Perhaps they read His will in a book.)
As everyone with half a brain knows,
we, each and every one of us,
create God in our own image.
And images, we all know,
are false gods, idols.

A cat knows nothing about King Arthur.

7

How do we know?
If we do "know," how do we know
that this knowingness is, indeed,
how things are?

We come into this world "knowing" something,
something that feels true to us no matter what.
For some, it's Oneness.
Others: God's will.
Others: there's just this; nothing else.
Others: life after life.
Others: we're here to learn lessons.
Still others...
On and on we go.

As I see it,
all we have is the Unknown.
Not memories or remembrances;
not past lives, not yesterday.
Moment by moment, we who are alive,
we enter the Unknown.

You say I repeat myself.
Very well, I repeat myself.
(As my friend Walt would say.)
Or perhaps that falling apple
hit me
a bit too hard on the head.

"Just one more thing...." as Columbo would say.

Don't go, please don't go!
they cried in their hearts,
those who adored the wise man,
those who hung onto his every word,
the singer of songs on the world's stage.
They had no idea, no idea at all,
of the singer's true identity;
as they had no idea
of their own true identity.

To future poets,
whoever you may be

You, too, in time
shall fade into history,
into the dim past,
however little,
however great your fame.

You shall be as a speck of light,
elusive as memory,
elusive as the Great Mystery,
humble as dust,
and proud as wind
blowing through the dreams
of those still sleeping,
bringing tears of recognition.

You shall be what I have been to you.

The Truth about the real truth

Wine comes in at the mouth
And love comes in at the eye;
That's all we shall know for truth
Before we grow old and die.
—William Butler Yeats

If you want the truth, I'll tell you the truth:
Listen to the secret sound, the real sound, which is inside you.
—Kabir

We see and read the claim almost everyday,
"The real truth about..."
(You fill in the blank.)

"The American people have spoken."
This speaker does not speak for me,
and am I not an American?
"The whole world is watching."
I'm not watching and am I not part of the world?
"I promise you everything will be OK."
A movie cliché.
"I found love again..."
We do not find love. We find someone,
a creature, a place, an object, an idea,
something to give ourselves to.
For we *are* love.

How many other Big Lies
do we swallow each day,
nodding our heads,
not thinking?

Religion, looking for truth in a box,
in a book labeled Ancient Scripture.
Politics, looking for truth in money and power.
Poetry, in lines and images.
Science, in reason and technology.
Astrology, in the movement and mathematics
of the planets.
Psychology, in symbols and dreams.
Movies, in fiction and the box office.
History, in the past and relics.
Lovers, in each other and the future.
Sherlock Homes, after eliminating the impossible.
The Nobel Prize, in achievements and greatness.
Judges, in the law and public opinion.
Lawyers, in sympathy and closing arguments.
Skeptics, in just the facts, ma'am.
Doctors, in the body and mind.
Spiritual seekers, in a Master,
within
and without.
Each one, all of us,
guided by faith and imagination.

We live in a make-believe world,
like Gaius Julius Solinus of old,
in his *Collectanea Rerum Memorabilium*,
we eschew facts for the fabulous,
we twitter the world with fantastic scenarios,
conspiracies, surrealistic dreams,
private nightmares, scientific theories,
flights of imagination,
all the unresolved emotions
within the universe and within each of us.

What is the *real truth* about anything?
What is the *real truth* about a stone, a leaf, a door?
How do we *know*?
Not by what we see and hear.
(Witnesses to a crime,
each may tell a different story.)
Not with the ego.
Not with the thinking brain
that schemes and gathers facts
to support this or that premise.

We know with the Heart—
the center of our being,
the center connected to all centers.
Yet the Truth for you means *your truth*;
my Truth means *my truth*.
And, that, dear friends,
is a hard truth to embrace.

Turning 70

for Michael and Shanti

Celebrate, celebrate!
Raise your glasses high,
your wine glasses filled with delicious promises,
elements of the earth and creation—
sun, water, air, and soil.
Drink in the earth, the stars and planets,
drink in the history of this wine,
red, like the blood that stains the earth,
century after century.

Or, if you so choose,
raise white wine to your lips;
wine that contains, don't you know,
the subtle shimmering of angel wings.

Drink pure water if you wish.
Not city water!
Not bottled water!
Drink mythical water springing from the earth:
an ancient fountain for all to drink,
sweet, flowing, connecting each of us.

Whatever your taste, raise your glasses high
and celebrate this day, this time,
as I enter my 70th year of life on this planet.

2

We do not know each other?
Does it matter?
Celebrate your own life.

It's all history, this poem;
no matter the form.
What you read, you see and read as history,
time long past,
time never to come back again.

History, as usual, isn't very pretty.
A traveler who litters the road with garbage,
without thinking or caring, but just keeps going.
Or a kid with shiny rubber boots,
a kid who stomps and splashes a mud puddle,
just to see the splash.

So we want a good story.

Every story—your story—
every poem—this poem—
contains someone's history,
as the *Odyssey* contained Homer's story—
a history that invites you in,
for a moment,
and takes you away, for a moment,
from your own history,
as the story becomes part of your history.

Don't hesitate!
Allow your story to unfold.
Love your life, this life.
Know that death,
as part of your history,
may, at any moment,
without apology or explanation,
bring your story to an end.
In your version, that is.

Others may well keep their story of you going,
changing this, altering that.
Even improving your story perhaps,
with a lie or two.
Wouldn't that be grand?

3

Hopeful, naive, foolish,
time after time
fortunes and misfortunes have marked my life
and the life of my friends.

We expected the world to evolve,
to transform from hatred, stupidity and jealousy,
into tolerance, compassion, forgiveness.

I read in the newspaper today,
oh, boy,
that our galaxy,
seen from the farthest galaxy that appears
in the sky,
hasn't even formed yet.

So someone has to do it,
create the story that will transform our weapons
of mass destruction into towers of peace,
fear into love;
to transform the shadows into caresses.
So let it begin now, this moment, with you.

My companions and I, we're not a movement;
only an energy in movement.
We're not a revolution nor an evolution,

a political party or a social club.
Let me emphasize,
we walk together and we walk alone,
each of us.

Come, come, if you will,
I invite you.
Come, Friend, whoever you are.
Walk beside us,
                    into forever.

Looking back,
with a bottle of wine
& a grain of salt

Here I sit by the fireplace,
a man 70 years old,
delving into the archives of his mind.
Delving? Is that a contemporary word?
An old-fashioned word, no doubt.
As I am, no doubt.

The young,
do they understand memories
and the quickness of time?
Some do, I'm sure.
For you: this poem.
For those, who, like myself,
nudged by a bottle of wine,
a fireplace,
and a grain of salt,
who look back for a moment,
just a quick moment:
this poem.

Not in anger or regret or reconstruction;
not in sadness or fantasy or myth.
Just looking.
Just for a moment,
like discovering a batch of old love letters,
tied together with a broken string,
in a shoe box you had long ago tucked away
and forgotten.

We humans,
how we hold onto such tokens of love!

To grab the tiger
by the tail

To gather strength from the earth,
to reach upward into the heavens
and touch the sun,
to tuck its light onto the page
and into my heart!
Sometimes, yes, I hold not
starlight in my hands,
but moonlight,
allowing it's golden spell
to color my mind.
Either way,
sunlight or moonlight,
I will hold this light
before you
only for a moment,
only for a moment,
then I'm gone.

After the last line, *what?*
(4 billion atoms I'm told)

Your bones end up in the earth,
over time, like fossils, until they, too,
turn,
slowly, over time,
(but what do you care?)
into Mother Earth,
once again,
to bring forth new life,
another beginning, another chance.

Or they go up in flames.
Your loved ones, if you have loved ones,
they're left with a handful of ashes—
ashes they put in a precious box,
or perhaps a shoe box,
on the shelf,
like a beloved book they once read
or meant to read.

Age 30.
Enlightenment?
Anything can happen!
As I soon found out,
traveling in a foreign country.

Age 40.
You dance most of the night
to test the proverb.
You wear a new hat.
You wear lots of new hats.
You smile a lot.

Age 50.
You look over your shoulder,
your left shoulder.
Those are not your shadows looking back,
or so you think.

Age 60.
If you make it to age 60.
You look into a mirror.
You don't see anyone you once knew,
no one looking back.
You plant flowers on the earth.
You gaze into the heavens.
This time,
the sky above your head—
How beautiful the ever-changing clouds!

Age 70.
You see friends dying,
all around you, they're dying—
those still above the ground.
Some in pain; some in joy.
Most still asleep.

The years have come and gone.
Am I at peace?
Most of the time, yes.
If you don't ask about the barking dogs downstairs,
barking like politicians,
barking at the slightest hint of a threat.
Or the carpenter ants, invading our home
with its overcast view of city and mountains.

Or the wars, the murders and the stupidity
I read about daily, each day, in the newspaper.
Or the fact that I can't remember your name
or two things in sequence.
Or the bottles of wine,
like myself, shrinking in size.
The bottles of wine, I swear,
they look the same size as they once did,
a long time ago...but we know,
we know they're shrinking.

Be that as it may, whatever they say,
as you can see, here I am,
writing my last poem,
my last line.

Again.

Running streams

After all this time, these years,
70 years and counting:
the experiences, events, memories,
crimes and tragedies,
mistakes, missteps: all this history,
joy and pain, all the drama: all,
all shall settle to the bottom
like rich river soil,
to eventually, over time,
grow plants to feed the fish,
dragon flies and other insects;
and above this dark bottom,
we shall run,
we who have found forgiveness,
we shall run,
run like the stream, clear and free,
sparkling in the light,
the mirror of self-reflection
gone, no more:
twisted images, scarecrows
hanging in the wind.

Tonight, alone in the house,
I drink and I ponder this world

Perhaps, tonight, this long winter's night,
my rambling thoughts on the human condition
will sound as common as this red wine I drink.

(Forgive me, Mallarmé, if, in my youthful folly,
I preferred the impure *Les Fleurs du Mal*
and Blake's *Songs of Innocence and Experience*
to your cerebral and tortuous afternoons!)

I drink and ponder the mainstream corruption
of this passing world:
the fringe nuts; the unthinkers;
the unexamined premises
and our stinking rotten core beliefs;
the despair and angst of our lives;
love and marriage and family:
the full catastrophe.
The bankers, the politicians, the gangsters
in their dull-tinted limousines—
the same limousine that will run you down
when all you want is a fair shake.
The black spot on the rose,
the black spot on the lungs,
the black spot on the soul;
the hope until hope is useless;
the struggle to be real
in a self-delusional world of our own making.
"Where do we come from?
Who are we?
Where are we going?"

But what else is worthy of a man's thoughts?

Ah, wouldn't it be nice, my friend, to drink
exquisite tasting wine?
Wine made by an exquisite wine poet—
those $400 priced wines,
(in today's prices),
rather than this ordinary stuff I drink?

William Blake, at times, most times,
couldn't afford a bottle of wine.
Van Gogh couldn't afford paints and brushes.
Now, those who have the means to drink
such fine exquisite wines,
they praise Blake and van Gogh in museums
and in their private collections.
While, in the corner of their mouths,
they have no idea
what Blake could see in his garden,
or what van Gogh painted with such frenzy.
No idea, no idea, at all.

Growth of a kangaroo court

for Christopher Byck

Growth is a Kangaroo Court
by Douglas Blazek
An Atom Mind Publication, 1970.
18 pages; price: 50¢

On my copy of *Kangaroo*, on the inside cover,
Douglas writes:
"Don—Read then burn!
Sorry I let this one out.
Poem 5 years old and like another man's rubber.
All without meaning to any of us now,
tho at one time it served a purpose.
Have since rewritten (ah-hum) and even tho it is
still sans meaning
to us,
at least it now isn't as embarrassing in a technical
sense."
Douglas Blazek
Oct. 1971

Ah, those were the days.
But we moved on, Blazek and myself.
Kryss and Willie, too.
Now, a few years later, with the appearance of the
Internet,
a man wants to sell *Kangaroo,*
a copy with a "slight coffee stain on the spine."
Price: $48.00.

Ah, Blazek, my friend, perhaps the coffee stain
on the spine of your book—
the book you said to read and burn—
perhaps this coffee stain looks like Jesus
or the Virgin Mary;
or perhaps a Robert Crumb drawing—
such as the one on your book
Zany Typhoons.

Or perhaps this stain reveals an image of God.

Yes, that's it!
The god called Moolah.
The god of whom we most slavishly praise,
from sea to shining sea,
from the Columbia to the Potomac,
to the 24 k highways of Heaven.
Moolah! Moolah! Moolah!

In praise of small things

Can we agree a key
is such a small thing?

Perhaps the key is money,
a credit card;
a gun; a shovel.
A bone for the dogs,
or a red wheelbarrow.
Perhaps the key is kindness:
a key that opens your heart
to forgiveness.
Perhaps a ticket
you hold in your pocket:
a ticket to a movie,
or a lottery ticket worth millions
of opportunities, millions of headaches.

Or perhaps you're young and beautiful,
perhaps even talented or a genius:
a key that takes you down,
down the yellow brick road,
in a limousine, no less,
until it doesn't.

For some, the key might be the body.
For others, the mind;
For still others, the imagination,
or psychic insight; or spirit;
or essence.
A stone in the middle of the road.
A leaf. A flower. A door opening.
Even a ritual will serve as a key.
Or perhaps the law, or mercy,
if you're forgotten the spirit.

Life: death: both keys that serve us,
to remind us what we truly are.

Singing in the morning, singing in the afterlife

for Zada, 1928—2011

The birds
singing in the early morning
outside my window,
when I was a boy
growing up in the South,
and now, after all these years,
now that my hair has turned white,
the birds singing
in the early morning outside
my window,
as I lie restless and unsleeping
next to my love,
as she dreams in her sleep,
her peaceful sleep—
no doubt these birds shall be singing
long after my own voice,
and your voice,
whispers into a ghost,
and like the proverbial tree
in the woods
falling
into unfathomable silence.

Or shall our voices ride on solar winds,
merging with all voices
into the singing hum of the universe?

319

Only so many mornings, only so many evenings

Imagine, if you will....
—John Lennon

Imagine a single cloud in the sky.
All day, a single cloud.
Every day.
A single cloud.

Imagine only one bird singing.
Each morning, one bird
singing outside your window.
One bird,
signing the same song
in the forest,
over and over on a single tree,
the only tree in the forest.

Imagine no seasons
but only one continuous season.
No need to change summer to winter outfits.
No need to change your mind
or your opinions.
You could hold the same beliefs forever.
You could repeat the same action
over and over,
each day, every day.
A fundamentalist paradise!

320

Imagine a song stuck in your memory.
The same song.
For days, months, years, over and over.
The same song singing in your head.

Now imagine knowing only one book.
Your entire life, only one book.
Say, Homer's *The Odyssey*.
Or the *Koran*.
Or Lao Tzu's *Tao Te Ching*.
Perhaps the *Torah*,
or the Christian's *Holy Bible*.

Imagine living your life believing
only
one view of the world.
A single version.
Be it a world filled with Cyclops,
monsters in the sea
or in the basement of your mind,
or rules telling you how
to live your life—
rules not made by you,
but by another
in the name of still another.

Imagine,
when it comes your time to die,
who will die in your place?

Dreaming,
just dreaming

Milosz, you sing of a lost century,
a forgotten name of a classmate—
a woman, who, after all these years,
comes to you in a dream,
arousing you,
as, no doubt, women have appeared
in men's dreams
since the beginning of time.

As I dream now and then of a woman,
lost in her own dream;
a woman just out of reach,
as always,
just out of reach,
dissolving into the light.

Only now, this moment,
at peace
with another dream,
I look out my window facing
Mt. St. Helens
to watch the wood smoke
curling
into the air
from a neighbor's chimney,
this early spring morning,
as I wait for my love,
now awake,
to descend the staircase
and enter,
as only a woman,
barefooted in her own dream,
enters so gracefully,
our kitchen,
for her morning coffee.

Tombstones after all these years

If you look carefully,
you'll see an ordinary looking man,
staring into space,
no thoughts on his mind.

Out of the blue,
as they say,
this ordinary looking man breaks out
of his Ulysses' gaze,
allowing Heart to oversee
the waves and particles streaming
through his mind.

A word comes forth.
Then another.
An image that rings in the air
like a gong chime—
a thought that sparkles his eyes
like the first flash of lightning in a dark sky,
followed by a rolling thunder of words
that sound around and around the world,
perhaps even to the stars,
shattering mirrors and thrones and theories,
brushing past remnants of Theia
and the Big Bang,
as these words journey homeward.

And you, silent
as the turning of the earth,
you watch and witness this cosmic reflection,
as fan blades whirl around and around
casting a shadow

on the ceiling above your head.
A dog barks then wags its tail.
An African violet blooms before your eyes.

An ordinary hot summer's day.

A zillion poets caught in a net of words.
For some, stepping stones into the illusory world.
For others, tombstones on the way out.

Do we really change?
Or do we simply change outfits in a mirror?

Round and round goes the moon

for William Hageman

It was late in November,
as they well remember,
that I was born in the early morn.

Or so they tell me,
and who I am to disagree?

To be born, what does it mean?
To die, what does it mean?
Books, proverbs, religions:
just shadows we peer through;
a ghost in the curve of our eyes;
and in the distance everywhere,
sirens,
just before a screeching halt,
a STOP sign, a wall, a mirror
splintered into a thousand images.

**This moonlight tour—glitter,
flash and novelty—arranged
for you
by
"WE SEE WHAT WE WANT TO SEE."**
Eye lashes won't protect you,
nor another city, another tour,
however much you're worth
or whose bare legs
you reach to move upward.

Round and round goes the moon.
Hang on tight or leap into the void?
An umbrella or a sword?
A romp through time.
Adam to the atom. Servants to our past.
We laugh when the Emperor laughs.

The halls of knowledge won't admit us.
A pure heart like pure poetry eludes us.
Tangled in speech and impure genetics,
like birds
caught in protective netting,
we go round and round with the moon.

You can't make sense of it
cause
it doesn't make sense.

We fall spiraling into our own dream.

**Welcome
to the land of *Youkali*.**

Stretching to touch you, relaxing in the flow.
Nowhere to go.

What to do? How to say?
Like sunken ships, centuries
lie scattered in the subterranean folds
of my mind.
I feel these centuries,
here, in the curve of my own time.
They do not surface as lost treasures
found. Or Kubla Khan visions.
Or quantum dreams.
They ascend on waves of feelings.

Lilly Poo, our mini dachsie,
barks with the bark of her breed,
stretching back to her line's origin.
My mind stretches before the beginning.

But what does this mean to you?
Or to Janie, sick with a cold,
concerned about her immigrant students.
(Some illegal, of course.)
Or concerned over her changing looks,
and looking for fullness in her grandkids
and generations beyond.

What do I say to you?
And to a universe
that will someday no longer be?

God speaks to me

God the Great Mystery
God the Great Unknown
God All That Is
God That I Am
—David Pendarus

God speaks to me through all living things,
through the ragweed on the roadside
and the hosta in my garden,
through the rain that showers down out of the blue,
and the sun that appears to come and go each day,
and the waxing and waning of the cyclic moon.

God speaks to me through the harsh winds
that blow down the Columbia Gorge in wintertime
toward our house;
and through the gentle breezes of May,
as I go walking in the cemetery across the street
with Lily, our piebald dachsie.

God speaks to me through the barren trees
in my neighbor's yard,
and through the green grasses in our yard
where Lily darts out to pee.

God speaks to me through all living things.
Can anything that lives truly die,
but only change form?

God speaks to me as Lily runs in circles
round the living room floor,
and as she chews on the bones she so loves.

God speaks to me through the garter snake
in our garden,
a timid creature that, nevertheless,
terrifies my Janie.

God speaks to me through the lady bugs
that, to my mind,
never feed enough on the aphids that feed on my roses,
and God speaks to me through late autumn spiders
spinning these fine garden webs that I curse
when running smack into them face first.

God speaks to me in the waters of the earth,
in the fire within,
and in the moving sky,
in the wind dancing through the leaves,
and in the quietness of a stone.

God speaks to me,
not in churches or mosques or candled shrines
on the side of a well-traveled road.
Not in the written word. Or in sacred scriptures.

God speaks to me
not through death but through all living things.

Whose child is this?

Enclosed in this bubble of existence,
longing for a home we cannot name
but only feel,
we seek refuge in words and images.
We seek refuge in idols.
We seek refuge in drama.
We seek refuge in the other.
We seek refuge in things.
We seek refuge in nature.
We seek refuge in beliefs.
We seek refuge in God.
We seek refuge in the illusion
we call self.
On and on,
we seek refuge in all that we do
and think.

Evening sun bright through dying leaves.
A dog chewing on a bone.
A man reading a poem.
Silence. Only sound a cracking bone.

This moment.

Let the story begin
Out of our dreams, comes the world

Worlds collide
They intersect
They war each other
Embrace each other
Dancing, dancing, a great dance
Dancing the dreamer's dream
Here
There
Everywhere at once

Just out of the womb,
8-1/2 minutes,
(Or was it 84?),
I looked around:
"What's going on?"

2

"I'm not a shape shifter!"
he testified to the philosophers,
the religious, the skeptics, the seeker,
to anyone who would listen.
"I'm a shift shaper."
His friends called him a loose marble
rolling around in the mind of God.

3

The shift between worlds
lasts but for a split,
then we enter a hazy zone,
a veil, a time and space
in which neither rhyme nor reason
prevail.

331

"Show. Don't tell!"
the poets cry.
Shall we deny the dying
of the light?
When our images evaporate
into thin air
like the ember rays of sunset,
are we to say,
"That's all, folks!
The show's over! Go home now.
Go home. Go home."

Already this world is a memory
to me.
Now I must continue
on my journey.

4
"Remember,
listen to the trees,"
a spiritual master told her daughters,
just before she passed.
"Listen to the trees. Talk to the flowers.
Float with the clouds.
Know that you are loved
whoever you are,
and dance your destiny,
dance your life in its wholeness.
Remember who you are."

For you

For those who long for the lights of home.
For the crazed ones who live in the shadows.
For lovers, everywhere.
For you,
whoever you are.
May you carry on with kindness
in your actions
and may you know forgiveness
in your heart.

This Passing World/
Journey from a Greek Prison

If the poems and stories in *On the backs of seahorses' eyes* have meant anything to you, please check out Don Cauble's first published novel: *This Passing World*. Available in eBook, paperback and hardcopy versions.

www.thispasingworld.com

§

On his honeymoon in Greece with his lovely bride Angelina, David Pendarus, through his own willful actions, finds himself in prison, along with drug smugglers, murderers, rapists, and thieves. He then begins to take a relentless look into his past and his intense and painful romantic entanglements—a journey, like Odysseus, full of twists and turns—in order to answer one burning question: Who am I? *This Passing World* tells the story of one man's journey to free himself from the prisons—within and without—of his own making. The characters and setting are vivid and alive. The time emerges from the depths of forgotten memories: everything rings with a universal chord, for we have all been prisoners of something once. How does one transcend? *This Passing World* suggests a way and leads us gently by relating the characters' experiences.

Thoughts on *This Passing World*

Cauble spins detail with a precision that suggests real-life familiarity, fleshing out the characters into believable, relatable people. He connects far-flung players—artists, musicians, fellow nomads, Greek villagers, drug smugglers. David Pendarus is a seeker with the flexibility of a willow branch...What begins as the story of his marriage to his beloved Angelina, unfolds into a meandering journey across spiritual and physical worlds...and, ultimately, to a Greek prison.
  —*Kirkus Review*

*****

This Passing World kept me turning pages. The book falls somewhere between a memoir and a novel. It drifted along in a very loose way, but as it went, something intangible began to gel, and characters took on more and more dimension. It's that something intangible that is always the hallmark of a good book.
  —*John Bennett, Hcolom Press*

*****

THIS PASSING WORLD. I read it, and passed through your window into another world. Nice work.
  —*Jeff Maser, bookseller,*
  http://www.detritus.com/maser

*****

Don Cauble had the misfortune to be in Greece during the time of the Colonels. For a mere handful of weed, he was sent to prison for two years. This book recounts the years before, during and after that time with fluid prose and poetry that makes it a pleasure to turn the pages.

Cauble's insights into the places he lived and the women and men he encountered, find a place in the reader's mind as if he had accompanied each scene and person with an indelible photograph.

Cauble's generosity of spirit allows him to portray a time of ecstasy and privation with a calmness (sometimes hard to maintain) grounded in his understanding that nothing you do, or that happens to you, can alter your essential self.

Elsewhere he has said: "My writing attempts to show how consciousness reveals itself, by shifting time—sequences, events, perceptions—to suggest that everything is happening at once, simultaneously."

　　—William Hageman (the Willie),
　　somewhere in Australia
　　Author: Living in the O

*****

For poet and sometimes philosopher David Pendarus, the central character in *This Passing World*, that life-altering experience was a two-year stretch, from 1972-1974, in a Greek prison. The arrest came at an especially inopportune moment, during an extended honeymoon in Greece. Pendarus' relatively carefree life of literature, poetry, travel, adventure, and romantic love ended abruptly in the isolation of jail cell in a foreign land. Deprived of freedom, thrown in with a group of international ruffians, robbers, murderers, and ordinary outlaws, not to mention those poor souls swept up in the dragnet cast by a repressive, despotic military junta, Pendarus is forced to reconsider his life, to examine closely the people, circumstances, and choices that brought him to that Greek slammer. Most importantly, he was forced, or afforded the opportunity, to ask that most important philosophical and spiritual question: "Who am I?"

Beneath and above all the sometimes confused, sometimes desperate, sometimes painful, but always hopeful searching for new ways of connecting with each other, most of the men and women in *This Passing World* are deeply concerned with finding an authentic, viable form of spirituality, something different, more real, more meaningful, more relevant than the institutional forms of religion they grew up with. Beneath all the drugs, the sex, the music, the radical politics, was an earnest desire to find a transcendent dimension in our human life, something that gives meaning and purpose to an individual life. The characters in this novel are spiritual seekers, especially David Pendarus, the imprisoned Odysseus of this journey of spiritual discovery. Yes, they were mostly unconscious and unaware of that fundamentally human urge, and yes, sometimes, even usually, they looked for love and truth in all the wrong places, but the motives are pure and sometimes so were the results. Sometimes these seekers found, more or less, what they were looking for.

Some readers may dismiss the forms of spirituality in *This Passing World* as impossibly New Agey, but if they look more deeply, they will see that the searching and the discoveries of the characters in the novel are not all that different from more conventional religions. Is David Pendarus' authentic spiritual experience in that jail cell in Greece essentially different from that of Saul/St. Paul on the road to Damascus, or the Buddha's enlightenment beneath the fig tree 2,500 years ago, or the illumination of Jesus on the cross, or the earth-and-heaven shattering spiritual experiences of hundreds, perhaps thousands of mystics from around the globe and in every century? I don't think so. The language of literature, especially poetry—both present in this novel—is basically the same, pointing to a Light that transcends the cares, concerns, sorrows, suffering, and sadness of this passing world of shadows, this dream within a dream, while at the same time infusing everything in that very world with its Truth. We are, as I've heard it said, not human beings having a spiritual experience, but spiritual beings having a human experience. In the end, we are indeed all Beings of Light.

—From a review by Larry Setnosky, artist in wood

§

Full Disclosure

To paraphrase the philosopher David Hume, on his publication of *A Treatise of Human Nature*, Cauble's book, *This Passing World*, "fell stillborn from its publication, without reaching such distinction as even to excite a murmur among learned writers, except for a few poets and friends."

About the author

Don Cauble grew up in the South and received an MFA in Creative Writing/Poetry from the University of Oregon in 1966. He has lived in San Francisco, Greece, and Denmark, and now lives in Portland, Oregon. He's an avid gardener.

"The details of my personal life matter little. What matters is who I am in relation to the timeless. My writings are an attempt to answer the question: Who am I? To follow this question is take the journey of your life. It is the journey that will lead you to the source of your being (and the Source of all that is)."
—Don Cauble

A list of books Don Cauble has authored appears on page 2 of this book.

This Passing World is his first novel.

How to order this book

Copies of this book can be ordered from
Amazon.com.
For printed copies signed by the author,
please visit www.seahorseseyes.com
Click on the "Order" tab, and follow the instructions.

You can contact the author by writing to him at
seahorseseyes@gmail.com

To read excerpts from his novel
and to order
This Passing World / Journey From a Greek Prison
please visit www.thispassingworld.com